H, My Name Is Henley

Also by Colby Rodowsky

H, My Name Is Henley

Colby Rodowsky

FARRAR STRAUS GIROUX
NEW YORK

For Stephen Roxburgh

H, My Name Is Henley

one

H, my name is Henley.

That comes from a school I went to someplace along the way. Wherever it was, all the girls were into jumping rope at recess. Not just jumping, but reciting this verse that went, "A, my name is Alice, I come from Alabama, and I eat apples." Then on to B, C, D— The trick was to get all the way to Z without missing. Not right away, of course. It took practice. And time.

Time was what we didn't have much of. We moved a lot—Patti and I.

I got to just past the middle of the alphabet when we were off again. The trouble was, at the next school everyone was playing stickball.

Where we were now was Baltimore, in an apartment with a toad on the ceiling.

It wasn't really a toad—just a water stain that looked

like one, and the gray, gritty surface of the ceiling seemed to splash around it like swamp water.

"Toad-ugly," I thought, looking up at that blotch, then down again, and hoping that in the time between looking and not looking it had turned into something else. A dragon, or maybe a unicorn.

But it was still a toad.

Some things I can do something with—change them, or make them over—if not in real life, then at least in my head. The best of the turned-into things, I put in my journal, which is one of those black-and-white marble copybooks that look boring on the outside. But that's okay, because it's what is on the inside that matters. Like me. I figure on the outside I'm basically square-shaped and sand-colored. But inside—inside, I like to think I'm wind chimes and drum-rolls and a big brass band.

Patti says that maybe the time will come when I care about the outside of things, too.

I doubt it.

Patti is my mother, and if she were the only person around, I wouldn't have to have a boring-looking journal, because Patti doesn't read other people's journals, or mail either.

But to get back to the toad. I can see it when I'm lying flat on my back in bed, the way I was that Sunday morning. What I did then was what I always do when that toad starts to squirm. I flopped over on my stomach and bunched the pillow on top of my head and thought about all the cracks and splotches and stains on all the ceilings in all the worn-at-the-elbow places we'd ever lived. How those cracks and splotches shaped themselves into bears, parrots, and one-

4

eyed jackals that seemed to clump along after me wherever I went. The way I clumped along after Patti.

Then I inched the pillow away from my head and peeked up at the ceiling. There he was—the gray toad glowering down at me. I must have been getting used to him, because all of a sudden he looked okay. Toad-ugly and all.

He was toad-ugly the way the whole apartment was toad-ugly, starting with my room, which was so small that sometimes, when I stood in the middle and stretched my arms and legs out in all directions, I wondered how long it would take for me to grow enough to be able to touch all four sides at once.

The room, with windows on three sides, had been called the sun parlor when the house was a real house and not split, top to bottom like an English muffin, into two apartments. It was followed by the living room, and after that, through a doorway with a beaded curtain, came Patti's room, and then the kitchen. Four rooms in a row.

Toad-ugly, and I liked it.

Then the smells got to me: the stale smoke and the leftover party smells that seemed to have crept under the bottom of the glass-paneled door, past the grungy gauze curtain that was bunched top and bottom along the rod, and into the room.

That's when I jumped up and knelt at one end of the bed and pushed the windows open. For a while I just leaned there and felt how it was really spring and listened to the Sunday sound of church bells and barking dogs and watched Mrs. Goodman coming down the street carrying a large white bakery bag.

"Hey, Mrs. Goodman—you know what?" I yelled as she got closer. "If I wanted to, I could spit right on your head."

"Know what, Henley?" Mrs. Goodman called back. "If *I* wanted to, I could spit right in your eye. Want a doughnut?"

What I like about Mrs. Goodman is, she'll tell you she's going to spit in your eye and offer you a doughnut all in the same breath. That's okay.

"Ummmm, yum." I leaned all the way out. "Are they jelly?"

"Sure thing," said Mrs. Goodman, reaching into her bag and handing me one. "Where's your mother?"

"Patti's asleep. But when she gets up we're going someplace. Maybe out to breakfast. Or lunch. Or someplace for the day."

"Good," she said, reaching back into the bag and holding out two more doughnuts. "Here you go. Take these for when Patti wakes up—while you're deciding what to do."

That's what I mean about her being okay. Mrs. Goodman never acts as if she thinks Patti and I are different or anything.

I went into the living room and put the doughnuts on top of an empty pizza box and sat cross-legged on the couch. I remembered lying in bed the night before and hearing the sound of laughter, the rattle of glasses, and feeling sort of empty—the way you get from listening to someone else's party. I remembered called goodbyes poking into my sleep, and the sound of voices on the street outside the windows of my room.

Sniffing at the dregs in the bottom of a wine glass, I picked up the burnt-out matches one by one and dropped them into an empty beer can, glad that nobody had stayed over, sleeping on the couch or the floor or curled onto the bean-bag chair. Glad that none of Patti's friends was still there this morning, staying through the day and maybe into the next, the way they sometimes did, so that I had to step over and around them—never sure how many there would be for supper.

But today was for us. Patti had promised.

Suddenly Patti was there. Standing tangled in the beaded curtains and rubbing her eyes, her yellow T-shirt barely covering her bikini pants. "What a mess," she said. "Let's get out of here. Let's *do* something."

"It's warm," I said.

"Really warm?"

"*Really* warm."

"Then let's eat out back," said Patti, shrugging at the cluttered living room and drifting on through the kitchen, out the back door. I watched her settle on the top step in a patch of sunlight, pulling her T-shirt down over her knees until she looked like a giant mushroom. "How about some coffee?" she called back over her shoulder.

I put the kettle on the stove, poked at the empty coffee mugs and beer cans in the sink, found the lid to the pickle jar, emptied the ashtrays into the trash bag, all the time trying not to gag at the stale, burnt smell. I put a mug of chocolate milk on a tray for myself, shaking some instant coffee into a mug for Patti and adding Mrs. Goodman's jelly doughnuts. I poured the boiling water into Patti's mug, crossing my fingers for something magic to happen as I dumped the rest into the sink and watched the steam poof up around me—hoping the hot water would wash away the glasses, plates, and soggy cheese curls that lay there like yellow worms. The air cleared but the mess was still there. So much for crossed fingers.

Kicking the door open, I took the tray outside. "You ought to put something on," I said as Patti reached for the coffee. "That old guy next door *looks*."

"So let him look. Besides, what's to see?" Patti tugged at her T-shirt. "I'm covered down to my toes."

"But, Patti . . ."

"But, Henley," said Patti, stretching her legs out in front of her, wiggling her toes so that her red-painted toenails caught in the sunlight. I hate red toenails.

"You're my kid, not my mother," she went on. "My God! As if I didn't have enough of that at home. 'Patti do this' and 'Patti do that' and 'What will the neighbors say, Patti' and 'Pa-tri-cia . . .' Now, what do I have?" She held her coffee mug up as though she were making a toast. "What I have now is a middle-aged kid, that's what."

After a while Patti closed her eyes and rubbed her forehead, and said, "Sorry, sweetie—that didn't come out the way I wanted it to. But you are, you know. You're the only twelve-year-old I know who's going on forty-five."

I chewed on that doughnut until it was spit, licking the rim of sugar from around my mouth. Licking. Licking. Licking. Finally I asked, "How about Aunt Mercy? Did she do that? Tell you what to do and all?"

"Aunt Mercy," said Patti vaguely, staring out at the alley in back of the house. "Aunt Mercy was for visiting. For summers and school vacations. As grown-ups went, Aunt Mercy was okay."

For as long as I could remember, Patti had told me Aunt Mercy stories. There were stories about how Aunt Mercy had gone off to medical school just after her young doctor husband had died. Stories about her house in the country with a front porch and a back porch, and front steps and back steps. Stories about how everyone in town knew her, and how she knew them, down to whether they had had measles or mumps, or even chicken pox. They were bigger-than-life and too-good-to-be-true stories. The kind of stories that Patti told me when I had a stomach ache or the flu. The kind of stories that I took to bed with me and told myself over and over again after the light was out. Mostly, I guess, because they came out of Patti's past and not from a book.

And once there had been a Booshie story: one that Patti told and then never told again. She said that she never remembered telling it at all.

"You know what I think," I said all of a sudden, looking away from Patti. "Sometimes I think there isn't any Aunt Mercy—that she doesn't really exist—that maybe the stories about her aren't really true."

"Don't be silly," said Patti, sliding down a step.

By then my heart was thumping so hard I was sure that at any moment it would rattle the steps. I pushed on.

9

"Then how come we never see her? How come there aren't any letters or birthday presents or . . . Mary Jane has a grandmother and . . ."

"Your one grandmother's dead. Before you were born. I told you that. You know about the other one. And Aunt Mercy . . . Aunt Mercy's busy . . . Besides, too many people would just slow us down. I've told you this before. How it's just you and me. Don't hassle me, anyway."

Patti jumped up, sending crumbs and sugar flakes showering down around her. "He's looking. That creep next door. Come on. We're going out. Someplace where we can enjoy the spring without a pervert. We'll go to the university—there's an outdoor concert. Come on."

Patti twitched her rear end as she started up the steps. Like a windshield wiper. Twitch. Twitch. Twitch. I thought about the grandmother I had never known and how she would say "Patti, don't do that . . . Pa-tri-cia . . ." I bit my lip and waited until my mother was all the way in the house and the screen door had slapped shut behind her, then I turned and stuck my tongue out at Mr. Barber as he peered out from behind his kitchen curtains.

The concert was in the quadrangle of the university, and all around us, people sat on blankets and old spreads and faded beach towels. There was some of everybody. Students, teachers, and families with picnic hampers. Old men and women from the apartment houses nearby who had brought lawn chairs and sat tapping their feet. Dogs on leashes and babies in strollers, and people forming dance squares on the edge of the crowd.

I leaned back on my elbows and held my face up to

the sun, closing my eyes and following one particular squiggle inside my lids until it curled and spiraled its way out of view. Then I turned and watched Patti as she sat on the table talking to a couple of guys doing something with a beer keg. I saw her jump down and start across the quadrangle, weaving her way quickly through the crowd, her peasant blouse and red skirt clinging to the front of her body and billowing out in back, and her shaggy, dark hair blowing straight out. Only there wasn't any wind.

"Come on, let's get out of here," she said, swooping past me without even stopping.

"Hey, wait." I jumped up and stepped off the edge of my clog. It got me right in the middle of the underneath part of my foot that hurts just to think about it. I hobbled along, calling "Wait up" as I followed Patti around the side of a building.

"It's dull," said Patti, back over her shoulder. "All those dreary people, and nobody much here today. And the group is—well, what you need, sweetie, is some discrimination. Come on. We'll do the museum instead."

"Don't call me 'sweetie,' " I said under my breath, hurrying to catch up.

We went along the side of Shriver Hall, past the parking lot where we'd left the car, through the sculpture garden and around to the front of the museum and up the steps, with Patti always two steps ahead.

"Can we see the mummies?" I asked, catching the heavy glass door before it swung shut, and thinking of the mummy story I had written one time after we had been to the museum—another museum, in another city. It hadn't really worked out. I mean, there was plenty of dialogue—mummies are okay on dialogue if you remember to put in every once in a while that they talked cotton-mouthed. It's the action that wasn't right. Mummies don't actually *do* much.

Patti was still out in front of me saying, "Later . . . later. There's a white show I have to see. Over that way."

"White what?" I asked, swerving around a roly-poly guard in a gray uniform.

"White white," said Patti, turning into a large gallery swarming with people. "Actually it's called 'On White'—look."

I looked as Patti swung her arm around the room. And what I saw were a bunch of canvases all over the walls. All white. All empty. All, as far as I could tell, the same. Except for their size. At first I thought a whole bunch of artists were going to come and paint stuff while we watched. It was as if all those canvases were just waiting for something to happen. Sort of like having a whole row of notebooks waiting to be written in. But then I figured out that this was it. What with everyone stopping in front of this canvas, or that one, stepping backward or forward, shading their eyes with their hands the way some people do when they look at pictures, then moving on.

Patti darted forward and sat tailor-fashion on the floor, staring up at the square white painting. I edged my way to the other side of the room, away from my mother, who was being stumbled over like a misplaced footstool.

I leaned on the doorframe and looked at an enormous white canvas on the side wall, trying to figure it out. I

moved forward to read the card pinned next to it—
"Hubbub." Only, the picture was blank. I finally got
around to thinking that I was supposed to create a hubbub
in my head and somehow see it on that white piece of
canvas. Then I wondered why they didn't give me some
paint and let me make my own. Anyway, then Patti came
along. I guess she was tired of being fallen over.

"Come on, sweetie. Enough. Let's see some Cézanne,
and the mosaics." And I took off after her, away from the
crowd, through a string of deserted galleries.

My shoes made a clopping noise on the floor, and the
faster I went, the louder they sounded. We swooped past
the miniatures in glass cases covered over with green velvet,
around bronze statues of ballerinas. We hurried down halls,
past mosaics and tapestries, without even stopping. The
only thing I could hear was my shoes sounding sharp against
the marble floors.

"Hey, Patti, you know what I think?" I said, gasping
and running to catch up with her.

"What's that?" Patti threw back over her shoulder.

Clop, clop, clop, clop went my shoes.

"You know what I think, Patti? You know what the
difference between us is?"

"No, what?" said Patti, swinging into the Great Masters
Gallery and on toward the American Wing.

"The difference is," I said, "for you it's the going
someplace that matters . . ."

Clop, clop, clop.

". . . and for me it's the being there that counts."

I went around another corner after the tail of Patti's
skirt and ran smack into a small, gray guard.

13

"Quiet in this museum . . . all that noise . . . racing along . . ."

He shook his finger at me and seemed to grow and swell before my eyes. Over his shoulder, I saw Patti's head bobbing back and forth. Then all of a sudden she had me by the hand and was pulling me out of the gallery, into the main lobby.

"Did you see him?" Patti gasped. "Just like a blowfish. Blowing up like a blowfish."

"Like a toefish," I choked.

"Go-fish."

"Snow-fish."

The two of us—together—exploded into laughter. And for just a minute it was one of those times you want to hold on to. Carefully. Like holding a soap bubble.

Then it was over and we went across the lobby, out the door, and down the shallow steps. We went past the stone lion, through the garden with the benches and the wire sculptures, and up the road to the parking lot. It wasn't until we were back in the car with the plastic seat cold against my legs, the car smelling of the half-eaten apple in the back seat, that I remembered we hadn't seen the mummies.

two

When we got back home, Patti reached into the mailbox and dug around until I could hear her fingernails scratching on the bottom. It was Sunday and we both knew there wasn't any mail. She was looking for a note from Eric, one saying he had been by and would be back later on. But there was nothing.

Eric was Patti's friend, only he hadn't been around for a while. The thing about Eric—no, I guess I should say the thing about Patti—was that I hadn't thought she thought Eric was terribly important. While he was here.

Inside, the apartment was cold. The water in the breakfast mugs and last night's glasses was cold. The Chinese food we bought for supper in its little white cardboard boxes was cold. Even the egg rolls, deep down in the crunchy middle part, were cold.

"We should have had pizza," said Patti, poking her fork at a gummy heap of chow mein on her plate.

"We should have come right home after we got it," I said, remembering how the cartons of food had felt less and less warm against my lap while Patti drove around and around, past houses and apartments, checking for familiar cars and lights in windows.

"Don't nag. I just went to a couple of places, just to see who was home. So we'd have somebody to eat with, somebody to talk to. Where is everybody? When Eric didn't come last night, I thought sure we'd see him today. God, it's been a rotten day." Patti slumped down in her chair and reached for a cigarette.

"Don't sm—" As soon as I saw the look on Patti's face, her eyes restless and shadowed dark, I bit the word in half and said the first thing that came into my head. "You know what, Patti? Know what we're doing in school tomorrow? We're going on a field trip, to the aquarium. Remember, you signed the permission. We're . . ."

"And tomorrow's Monday," she said. "Back to that rotten job that's stifling me. There's no creativity. No anything."

I guess I hadn't distracted her fast enough, but I kept going anyway. "We're going by bus and Mary Jane and I are sitting together and I'm packing two peanut butter and jellies and she's bringing the Tastykakes." Criminy. I sounded like some really little kid.

". . . know what it's like working for a bunch of insensitive clods. They promised me when I went there that I'd go somewhere."

"Some of the mothers are coming—and a couple of

fathers. And there's a new dolphin." Much more of this and I'd make myself throw up.

"I don't know how much longer I can stand it," said Patti, grinding out her cigarette in a lump of white rice. "They're at me all the time. Dress suitably for the office. You're late again. Patti, do this. Patti, do that."

"And after the trip we can do a report for extra credit and Mary Jane and I are going to do a play." I had pushed my voice up so high that my neck was beginning to ache.

"A lousy receptionist in an ad agency. That's not getting anywhere. They promised. Talked about a foot in the door. I don't *need* that job. I need to breathe. To grow." Patti jumped up and ran out of the kitchen and through her bedroom that had been the dining room when this was someone's whole house. I saw the bead curtains still swaying from the rush of Patti's going. Saw her pacing from one side of the living room to the other, bumping against a rocker and setting it rocking frantically. The next thing I knew, her foot had clipped an empty Wheat Thins box and sent it spinning across the room.

And then I forgot about trying to distract Patti and about the look on her face and the restless eyes and just shouted as loud as I could, "PATTI, DON'T QUIT THAT JOB. YOU PROMISED ME."

"And they promised me something," said Patti, swooping back into the kitchen with her hands full of dirty dishes. "They said I could get somewhere."

"But you just started. You've only been there a couple of months." I turned away from her and took all the dishes out of the sink one by one and set them on the drainboard while I cleaned the sink, filling it with hot, soapy water. I

17

lifted the dishes back into the water and said, "It's a good job if only you'd give it a chance."

"Don't lecture me," Patti screamed. "Don't—lecture—me," she repeated slowly. "Just like your father—so practical and smug. So ready to settle down. To give up. And when I left—took you and left, and you a baby—don't tell me they weren't glad. Probably danced all over town—except they wouldn't have. Too proper to dance. My God, that might have been fun. And you, Miss Worrywart, you should be glad I didn't leave you there."

I pushed my hands flat against the sink and let the water creep up around my wrists and wondered what would have happened if Patti had left me there, and I pushed harder against the bottom of the sink.

"And then what happened?" Patti's voice rose and went on. "I'll tell you what happened. He was killed in a highway accident." Patti tossed an empty plastic dip container across the kitchen and into the sink. I blinked at the sudden splash of soapy water.

"Nothing works out lately," she went on. "Not this tacky apartment with the stuffing coming out of things, and that dreadful one-of-ten-million print of *Blue Boy* over the bed. I hate *Blue Boy*. I positively loathe and despise *Blue Boy*." Then Patti burst out laughing.

I felt something inside of me let go, like a marionette when the strings go slack. I turned to look at Patti, who was leaning back on two legs of a kitchen chair, laughing and wiping her eyes.

"I hate *Blue Boy*, and what do I care. It's the big things that matter. Doing things—and having fun. And we do have fun, don't we? Sometimes, anyway." Patti bumped the front legs of her chair onto the floor and was suddenly quiet. She reached her arms out. "Come here, sweetie, and give me a hug. I really am a pain, aren't I?"

So I went and stood next to Patti and let myself be hugged and thought about how I hated the kind of touching that made you tighten up inside yourself, and held my wet hands out stiffly as I watched the water drip onto Patti's skirt, turning the red dark and splotchy.

"You know what I've been thinking, Henny-penny? That maybe it's time we moved on. Went someplace else for a bit."

"But, Patti, you promised. You said we'd stay here a good long time. Even after you left that job at the restaurant, and after you stopped selling in a store."

"Stultifying," said Patti, shaking the fortune cookies out on the table and lining them up. "Anyway, what I thought was . . . What I had in mind . . ." Patti stared down at the fortune cookies as if they might explode at any minute. "Well, there's always Aunt Mercy. I thought we might go see Aunt Mercy."

"Aunt Mercy," I yelled, throwing my arms around Patti and giving her a bear hug—this was the good kind of touching—and trying to ignore the little tug of certainty that Patti hadn't thought of Aunt Mercy until that very minute. "You've promised before, but we've never gone. I mean, can we really?"

"I said when the time was right—and maybe now is the time." Patti's voice took on a funny tightness as she rearranged the cookies on the table in front of her like pieces of a game. Shifted and rearranged them without looking up.

"Can we really go to Aunt Mercy's?" I asked, wanting

to jump up and down and run around the table—and wishing for once that I was the kind of kid who could do that sort of thing. "And we'll see her house and where her office is, and the beach and the water tower . . . and everything."

"We'll see it all," said Patti, picking up a fortune cookie and cracking it open. She fished the little piece of paper out and read it, then read it again and held it out to me. "See. I told you we should move on. It says, 'Go swiftly . . . like the wind.' Here, you try one." And she tossed a cookie to me.

"I'll save it. Read it later," I said, putting the fortune cookie in my pocket. "But what about Aunt Mercy's . . . about going. When do you think we will?"

Just then the doorbell rang. Patti ran her fingers through her hair and started for the door, calling back over her shoulder. "Don't start packing, for heaven's sake. It was just an idea, and things might work out here after all."

I heard the voices in the hall, the sound of people spilling into the apartment. I heard Patti's voice louder than the rest. "Am I glad to see you all. Where's everybody been? We drove by, looking. Come in, come in. Is Eric with you?"

Someone turned on the radio. I heard a chair being moved, laughter, the little zip of a beer can. Patti came into the kitchen with a gallon bottle of wine. "Nell and Arnie brought this. Are there any clean glasses?"

She stood for a minute, with her hands on her hips. "It's still a mess, isn't it? Oh, sweetie, will you clean it up for me? Please. And then run along to bed."

That was when I attacked the kitchen, scrubbing at

dishes and countertops and mopping up murky blops of water. And that kitchen fought back, as if it had a mind of its own. Things kept being undone as soon as I had them done. Nell came for ice cubes and stayed sitting there on the edge of the table; Arnie reached for an ashtray and toppled a stack of saucers back into the sink. Someone needed extra glasses and someone else needed a bowl for Fritos. Patti's friend Angel ducked into the bathroom off the kitchen and Sid leaned against the refrigerator and talked about meditation with a girl in lace-up boots—only he wasn't looking at her boots. Every once in a while, someone would talk to me and ask me about school and what was new (since last night?). Then they'd ask if there was any coffee or stuff to make a sandwich with.

I gave the table one more halfhearted swipe. I knew the kitchen was going to win. Then I stepped around Nell and wedged my way past Sid; I went through Patti's room into the living room, climbing over the group in a circle on the floor listening to a guy play the dulcimer. I went into my sun parlor–bedroom and sat on the floor, leaned against the bed, and said, "H, my name is Henley . . . H, my name is Henley." I still say that sometimes when I need to know who I am.

For a long time I sat that way, watching the shadowed shapes on the other side of the curtain, listening to the music of the dulcimer and the muffled laughter from the kitchen. I reached into my pocket for the fortune cookie, picked it open, took out the fortune, and ate the cookie before I remembered I didn't even like fortune cookies.

I shoved the fortune part into a crack under the baseboard without reading it.

three

I woke up quickly and then lay there. The way you do when you're trying to latch on to a dream you've just had before it slithers away. I kept my eyes closed tight and bit by bit the pieces came back to me, stringing themselves out, one after the other.

We were back in the museum with the blowfish guard shaking his finger at me and pointing to a canvas on the wall. It was a picture of Patti and Blue Boy, with the furniture from the apartment jumbled in back of them.

The scene shifted and I saw Patti through the dangling blue and yellow beads, lying on her bed, saying, "I won't get up. I won't go to that rotten job. I won't. I won't."

Then I saw myself swallowed up by newspapers, circling help-wanted ads with red Magic Marker and reading them to Patti, and to the blowfish guard, to Blue Boy, to Angel and to Eric. They all laughed out loud.

The dream started around again: the guard shaking his finger at me and everybody laughing, laughing, laughing. The newspapers were piling up around us.

Jumping out of bed, I ran into the living room. Then I stopped short, swaying over a body bundled in a blanket on the floor, and veered around someone huddled in a bean-bag chair. I swatted the bead curtain aside and pushed my way into Patti's room.

"Hey, Patti, come on. It's morning. The clock didn't go off."

"I don't want to get up," said Patti.

"Come on," I said, half looking at *Blue Boy* over the bed, and then back over my shoulder at the rest of the room in case the dream was hiding there.

The alarm buzzed and Patti reached out to turn it off. "Ye gods, what's the matter with you? It's barely morning," she said, pulling the pillow over her head and burrowing deeper into the covers. "And besides"—she lifted a corner of the pillow. "Be quiet. There're people out there and they don't have to get up or poke along to some two-bit job."

The pillow came down again and Patti disappeared.

"Who?" I said, sitting uneasily on the bed.

"Who what?"

"Who's out there?"

"My friend Margey—and her friend . . . what's-his-name." Her voice was muffled. Pillow-mouthed.

I pulled my feet up and stuffed them under the bottom of Patti's covers. "Do I know them, and why are they here, and why do we have to be quiet, and besides, you have to get up. It's Monday."

"You're nagging again," said Patti, still under the pillow.

"We—ll," I said, stretching the word way out. "Who *are* they?"

Patti bundled the pillow over and stuffed it behind her head. "What is this, the Spanish Inquisition? I *told* you, it's Margey. We went to college together, and she's Angel's cousin and that's how I met Angel and now she's here in town, with . . ."

"What's-his-name."

"They came last night with Angel and Sid, who had a sitter for Tommy, and they wanted to go home, but it was still *early* so I said stay and they stayed and Angel and Sid left and—you know what—nobody even missed them. They're from New York. Margey, I mean, and . . ."

"Yeah. I know."

"Anyway, I told them they could sleep in. Told them we'd tiptoe." Patti poked one foot and then the other out of the covers. "How about putting the water on for coffee. Okay?"

I got dressed with one eye on the clock and made Patti's coffee, prodding her along. I packed the peanut butter and jelly sandwiches for Mary Jane and me to take on the class trip and stepped around the bodies in the living room. I changed from my yellow shirt to my pink and then back again, and tried to eat a piece of toast, but it stuck in my throat. Checking the clock again, I called "Time." I was sure I was going to be late for school and the bus would leave without me, so I wouldn't get to go to the aquarium at all.

Part of me wanted to leave Patti there and go along without her. The other part didn't dare leave before she did—for fear Patti wouldn't go to work.

"Come on," I said, coming into the living room, where Patti was watching a sleeping lump in the bean-bag chair.

"Now, that's the way to live," she said. "Nothing to do. Nothing at all."

"Come *on*," I said, holding the door open. "I'll walk you to the bus stop on my way to school."

"If I could take the car, I wouldn't have to leave so early."

"Bus is cheaper," I said, following her out into the hall. "Hey, I forgot something. I'll meet you outside."

I waited until Patti went out the street door, till I could see her standing on the sidewalk. Then I turned back to the apartment and took one look at the sleepers in the living room before I slammed the door as hard as I could. So hard that the walls shook and the glass in the outside door rattled. So hard that from the inside—from a blanket or a bean-bag chair—came a muffled, angry "Keep quiet, will you."

Margey?

What's-his-name?

I hurried right home after school with the opening scene of my extra-credit aquarium report running around and around in my head. I had figured the whole thing out on the bus going back to school—while everybody else was going from 99 to 0 bottles of beer on the wall, except for the teachers and the parents, who were smiling in that tight-lipped way that looks like rubber bands.

I started thinking about what the animals and fish would do if they could take over, bring off a revolution or a coup like they have in those South American countries. Not like one of those smarmy toy-store stories where the dolls and the wooden soldiers carry on all night. In my play, I saw the dolphins being tour guides and the sharks working the concessions. The Portuguese man-of-war selling tickets; and turtles, porpoises, and barracudas doing the sightseeing. The people would be inside the tanks. I was okay on action this time but the dialogue was giving me trouble and I sent Mary Jane home and told her to try to figure how the shark would talk. If a shark could talk.

I was pretty deep in all that, so when I opened the outside door and heard a radio blaring a song from *Chorus Line*, it took me a while to realize it was coming from inside our apartment. That and the sound of feet sliding against the floor. I turned the key and pushed the door open slowly just as Patti swung around and glided down into a partial split, landing between two bulging trash bags.

"Henny-penny! You're home. Come and help," she called, waving vaguely at the living room.

I blinked my eyes at the skirts and jeans draped over the rocker, and the open canvas suitcase on the couch. Stepping over a knapsack, I dropped my books on the table next to a pile of towels and a box of Christmas ornaments. I reached past Patti's boots and an electric coffeepot to turn the radio down.

"Patti—what—why . . . I mean—"

26

"Don't scowl, sweetie. It puts lines on your face. Besides, it's exciting. Absolutely."

"What are you *doing* here? Didn't you go to work? Didn't you . . ."

"I didn't *not* go," said Patti, getting up and putting the stack of towels into one of the plastic bags. "I started out—even got the bus. I got as far as Mt. Royal Avenue and then I started thinking about that lousy job and how it wasn't going anywhere and what Margey said last night. Anyway, I got off that bus, hopped in a cab, and came right home and woke them up. You know what—they think it's a terrific idea."

"What's a terrific idea?" I asked, all the time folding and unfolding last year's bathing suit and being pretty sure I didn't really want to know.

"Us going to New York. You and me," said Patti, turning the radio back up and skimming across the living room.

"But, Patti . . ."

"Henley, don't 'But, Patti' me. We're going to New York and I'm going to *do* something. Nothing's ever going to happen to me here. We should have done this years ago. The really terrific thing about it is Margey says we can stay with them until we get a place of our own. We'll take the sleeping bag and . . ."

"But we have an apartment right here and we've paid rent. Anyway, what about going to Aunt Mercy's? You said . . ."

"I didn't really say—just maybe. Aunt Mercy's is dull. Stodgy and stuffy. This is New York I'm talking about. And don't you see, smartie, it's the end of the month and if we get out of here quickly we won't have to pay any more rent. Won't be here to pay it."

"But it costs money to go to New York and we don't have any money. I know because last week when you told me to get milk on the way home from school Mrs. Redman said to tell you to pay our . . ."

"Who does she think she is—talking money to you?"

"You do."

"You're my kid, that's why. She's got some nerve. I told you not to go there. I gave you money and told you to go three blocks over. Redman's sells stale bread, anyway."

"If there's no money for Mrs. Redman, I don't see how there's money for anything else."

"Stop talking Mrs. Redman," said Patti, holding an Indian print skirt up to her waist, then tossing it into the open suitcase. "It's like you have tunnels in your head, little poky gray tunnels, and you can't see past them. Money tunnels and 'do this' tunnels and 'don't do that' tunnels."

"But I know what there is," I yelled. "I know because I have to know. I know what you make and what you get from Social Security and that's all there is and now we owe money to Mrs. Redman and you're talking about going to New York and then what?"

"You don't know everything. There's something else. Something that makes it all okay. All just fine." And Patti drifted across the floor, her body swaying to the beat of the music.

"What something? Patti, what something? Tell me."

"There's something put away. Something special."

All of a sudden I felt as though I was sliding and

couldn't stop. "You mean—but that's my—the money my grandparents sent after my father was killed?"

"Your money? Conscience money, if you ask me. Not even an insurance policy for you when he died, just that Social Security and the thousand dollars his parents sent."

"But you always said it was for me. That it was put away until we needed it."

"This *is* for you, don't you see. Going to New York *is* for you. So you'll have advantages."

"I don't want advantages, and besides, that money was special."

"It's only money. Don't be so selfish. It's not even a thousand dollars anymore, what with this and that. Things keep coming up." Patti turned and pulled out a drawer, upending it on the sofa. I watched a spool of yellow thread roll across the floor and waited until it came to rest against the baseboard before I said, "What about school? I have this extra-credit report due and Mary Jane and I are going to write a play and . . ."

"My God, you're a spoilsport," said Patti, shoving a hair dryer into the corner of the suitcase. "They have schools in New York. Besides, the school year's almost over. Anybody else's kid had a chance to go to New York, they'd be thrilled. They'd love it. Probably sing and dance."

I reached out to turn off the radio and said, "I'm not anybody else's kid."

I woke up early the next morning, before the alarm clock went off or the first of the early-morning traffic could be heard on the street out front. I crept out of bed, pulled back the curtain on the door of the living room, closed my eyes, and held them tight. Afraid to look: hoping that the bags and boxes and accumulated belongings had disappeared.

They were still there: just the way Patti had left them when she finally wandered off to bed the night before, calling over her shoulder for me to lock the door and get a good night's sleep. That we were getting an early start tomorrow.

Now tomorrow was today and everything was still the same: the plastic bags stuffed with winter clothes and snapshots and papier-mâché flowerpots that Patti planned to leave locked in the car until she could send for them; the two canvas suitcases, already zipped, bulging and poking out in all directions; the blue nylon knapsack and the sleeping bag; the cardboard boxes of trash.

I thought, the night before, as I pawed through the things Patti had thrown out, that wherever we went I always managed to leave pieces of myself behind. Like a snake shedding its skin. Now, I really don't know much about snakes and a herpetologist would probably flip, but the thing I can't help wondering is how long before a snake runs out of skins. Sometimes I would see myself standing there with layer after layer gone: just me in my bones.

Talk about toad-ugly.

Last night, as I was rooting through the trash, I found my old report cards and the program from *The Nutcracker* ballet that I had planned to save forever, and my *Lion, the Witch, and the Wardrobe* book report. But when I pulled them out I saw that the dregs of a shampoo bottle had oozed all over them. They were green and slimy. I kicked the trash box across the room.

Dragging a straw basket out from under the bed, I began to pack it with all my special belongings. I wrapped my Snoopy bank in the brown argyle socks Mary Jane gave me for Christmas and put it in the bottom of the basket with my camera and my carved wooden box with my earrings and the sea-gull necklace inside. I added my cat calendar and my current journal and all the old filled-up ones—all as alike as a bunch of Little Orphan Annie's dresses. I had just stuffed my hair holders down inside when Patti flung the door open and said, "Come on. Let's go."

But as the morning inched its way along, I found out that going wasn't simply a matter of going. First Patti had to call Angel to see if she could leave our old orange Volkswagen with the leaf bags stored inside parked in front of her house until we got settled. Then she called several other friends to ask them to pass the word along that she no longer had the apartment and not to drop in, but that as soon as she got a place in New York they would all be welcome. I knew what she was really trying to do was get word to Eric that she was gone; that she wasn't waiting anymore for him to come back. I guess if I could figure it out, probably Eric could too, but I also knew it wouldn't be terribly hard for him to find us. If he wanted to.

I was just pulling things out of the refrigerator and dropping them into the trash when Patti started out to go to the bank.

"Hey, wait, you won't take all the money, will you?" I

called, running after her into the hall with a bowl of furry-looking lima beans still in my hand.

"Well, we'll need the money. Till I get a job, and besides, there's so much to do in New York—shows and galleries and restaurants."

I had that sudden slipping-out-from-under feeling again. "But we can't use it all. There has to be something left in the bank. For an emergency. In case anything happens."

"Oh, for heaven's sake, Henley. There won't be any emergencies. It's going to be okay. It's finally going to be the way it's supposed to be." Patti stopped and looked at me for a moment. "All right, worrywart. Fifty dollars. I'll leave fifty dollars for your emergency."

I hate being called "worrywart" almost as much as I hate being called "sweetie."

When Patti got back from the bank with the money, it was as though the trip had really begun. She counted it out, then counted it out again. She divided it into piles, hiding some away in her knapsack and the secret place in her wallet, and even gave me some to put in the carved wooden box in my basket. "There," she said, fastening her knapsack. "There's fun money and food money and train money and . . . You know what I feel like? Some kind of little old lady stashing money away in envelopes. That's what you do to me. Make me feel like a little old lady. Come on, let's go by Angel's and leave the car. She said she'd drive us to the station. Come on."

Part of me wanted to yell at Patti, wanted to tell her she made me feel like a nag. But instead I said, "Don't forget. You promised. I have to stop—at the school—to get my transfer cards and leave my books."

Patti was out the door, pushing a trash bag with her foot and dragging her suitcase. "Okay. Okay. But hurry— we don't want to miss the train."

Piling my suitcase, the sleeping bag, and the basket out in the hall, I went back inside the apartment. I stood for a minute in the living room, then checked the kitchen and Patti's room. I turned away, then turned back again, moving as though I was a sleepwalker, and looked up at the picture over Patti's bed.

"It's all your fault, Blue Boy," I whispered.

four

I pressed my forehead against the window of the Metroliner and held it there, letting the vibration of the train go down through my arms and legs to the very bottom of my feet. We were out of Baltimore, across the Susquehanna River railroad bridge, and on our way. Lickety-click, lickety-click. I tried to fix the rhythm of the train and hold it in my head. Lickety-click. Lickety-click. Lickety-click. Then the wheels seemed to be lifted up, to fairly skim the tracks before they settled into a pattern again. Lickety-click. Lickety-click.

We were heading north: away from all the things that had cluttered the rest of the morning. Away from busybody old Mrs. Willard, the school secretary, who had fussed and scolded, saying that she needed a couple of days to prepare the transfer cards and she wasn't just sitting there with nothing to do waiting for some kid to come in even if my mother had called, and why hadn't she called earlier anyway. I stood in front of the desk, shifting my books from one arm to the other, and I guess Mrs. Willard figured I wasn't going to move, because in a few minutes she was opening and closing file drawers and clacking away on her typewriter. She sighed a lot.

"Oh, Mrs. Fitzpatrick," Mrs. Willard called to the principal as she passed through the room. She folded the forms into an envelope and handed them to me as she said, "Here's someone who is leaving us. Leaving *today*." I saw her shape words in the air over my head the way grown-ups do when they are acting sorry for you. The way that leaves you feeling half naked. I didn't want to be felt sorry for.

"Henley's been here a whole year now," Mrs. Willard said out loud. Right away I knew what Mrs. Willard thought of kids who went to this school and that school and all the schools in between: she thought that really sensible people went to a school and stayed there until they had used up all the grades. She didn't know Patti.

"Are you moving? Changing school districts?" Mrs. Fitzpatrick asked, half sitting on the edge of the secretary's desk. "Is your mother . . ."

"Out in the car," I said, taking a step backward. "She called before. We're going to New York and . . . We're going right away. Today, I mean."

"Going to New York? How nice," the principal said in the kind of voice you knew meant she didn't think it was nice at all. In my head I dared her to ask *why* we were going to New York.

Mrs. Willard's voice slid into an easy singsong. "Maybe

35

Henley would like to go to her classroom to say goodbye to all her friends. I know they would want . . ."

I thought about Mary Jane, thought about her in a way I had tried not to think about her all morning long—or even the night before—and how I hadn't even called to tell her I was going. I thought of my half of the aquarium play that was never going to get done, and of Mary Jane figuring out how the shark talked, and waiting for me in the morning and after school; and of Mary Jane gradually not waiting anymore and finding another friend on the playground or in the cafeteria. The lump in my throat seemed to grow and grow until I was sure I couldn't swallow—or speak —or even breathe.

Mrs. Fitzpatrick and Busybody Willard seemed to close in around me, pounding at me with marshmallow words that said things louder than if they had shouted them.

"Be sure to come to see us sometime."

"You've moved around a lot, haven't you?"

"Stop by the classroom and say goodbye."

"Just as you were beginning to feel at home . . ."

"And your friend Mary Jane—I've seen you with her in the halls . . ."

Their awful gooey-in-the-middle words just kept going on and on and piling up around me until I couldn't stand them anymore and I took those books and pushed them right into Mrs. Willard's middle as hard as I could, and I turned and ran down the hall and out the door.

The train stopped in Wilmington, where a bunch of people got off and others got on and after a few minutes everything looked the way it had before—as if maybe the first group had just decided to get back on. To keep riding. As we slid away from the station, I stared out the window and a movie reel seemed to be uncoiling right there on the ground beside the track. Bits of the morning flashed by, one after the other, faster and faster as the train picked up speed. I saw Patti parking the orange Volkswagen in front of Angel's house, and Angel herself taking us to the station; Patti and me standing in the ticket line, arguing about trains while the man in back of us sighed and kicked his suitcase along. "We'll take the Metroliner, it's faster," Patti said. "The regular train's cheaper," I said. "Faster is better, and we want to begin." Lickety-click. Lickety-click.

Patti stood up and caught hold of the overhead rack as the train lurched. "Come on, sweetie, let's go to the snack bar and get a Coke."

The train bounced and clattered and racketed along, throwing me from one side of the aisle to the other, while up ahead Patti seemed to glide forward, scarcely holding on. I came to the end of one car and waited till she was all the way into the car in front. I stood there for a moment with my knees braced, my shoulder holding the door back, and watched the platform where the cars were coupled, zigzagging from side to side. Lickety-click. Lickety-click. Then I took a deep breath and raced forward, feeling all at once a rattle against my feet and a rush of cold air and a great surge of excitement that made me want to laugh out loud.

I shot into the next car and arrived with a rush, catching hold of the snack bar as the train lurched suddenly.

"Watch it," said Patti, reaching forward to steady the

gray cardboard box with the Cokes inside. "Let's take these back to our seats. You go first this time. And take the cheese curls."

"Oh no, I'll never make it. I just barely got here." But by that time Patti was pushing at me from behind and I began to feel excited, the way I do on a merry-go-round when the thing really gets going. With a grin that pulled all the way across my face.

"Sure you will. Let's go," said Patti.

And I went, letting myself run with the train, swaying and darting and propelling myself along, with my hands barely touching the backs of the seats. My feet skimmed the aisle and jumped the clackety place between the cars and a kind of bubbling welled up inside of me that made me say, "We're going to New York. We're going to New York," over and over and over again.

"We're going to New York," I said, flopping down into my seat and tugging at the bag of cheese curls with my teeth.

"No kidding," said Patti. "That's what I've been trying to tell you since yesterday. And all I got was 'But Patti this' and 'But Patti that.' "

"Are we *really* going to New York?" I suddenly felt that it might all vanish: the train, the fields streaking by outside, and the woman across the aisle with her canvas tote. I put a cheese curl on my tongue and let the yellow cheese flavor fill my mouth, then crunched it before it had a chance to soggy up. "Really?"

"Really truly," said Patti.

"And is it . . ."

"It is."

"Is what?" I asked.

"Is wonderful," said Patti, holding her plastic glass up in a toast. "It's going to be wonderful for us. Finally wonderful. And I'll get this terrific job, at NBC or CBS, or maybe one of the big magazines. *McCall's* or *Redbook*. We'll get an apartment and ride in a buggy around Central Park and go to plays," she said, putting her head back and closing her eyes.

All the way to New York I thought maybe this time Patti was right: this time it *was* going to be wonderful. All the way past Philadelphia and Trenton and Newark and down through a tunnel and into New York City, it was as though I had lifted up my feet and was skimming after Patti.

We spilled out of the train with our suitcases, knapsack, sleeping bag, and my straw basket, and right away we were caught by the crowd and carried up the stairs into the station. Then I just stood still, staring at the ceiling and the space and the rush of people. Patti pushed me along with the knapsack. "Don't stop. You'll be trampled. Just remember, in New York you keep on moving," she said.

We found an empty seat to pile our things on while Patti read the signs that told about taxis and subways, and I counted bookstores, candy stores, and restaurants.

"Come on, we'll get a taxi," said Patti. She slung the knapsack on her back, picked up her suitcase, and started off almost before I knew what was what. The suitcase clunked against my legs and the sleeping bag and basket bobbled off one another as I ran after her, through the main concourse and up the escalator to the outside.

I guess if it had been up to me we never would have

39

gotten a taxi. They came and were grabbed and left and more came. Then Patti darted forward, pushed her way in front of a man with a turban, pulled open the door, and called over her shoulder, "Come on. This one's ours."

Before I knew it, I was in the cab with my face pressed against the window, twisting my neck and trying to see the tops of things. "It's so—so—"

Patti gave the driver Margey's address, then leaned over to look out the window with me. "Yes, isn't it. So—and there're all these people and now there's us too and it's going to be fantastic."

The taxi stopped and started and stopped again. Horns blared, trucks roared down on us, buses gasped and sighed. People darted into the street and a siren wailed. I leaned back against the seat and pushed my feet out in front as far as they would go. "I'm in New York," I thought. "I am in New York."

The cab driver pulled up to the curb in front of a red brick apartment building with a green awning that had *New York University School of Law* along the side in stumpy white letters.

"No," said Patti, leaning forward. "This can't be right."

"Look, lady—you said 33 and this is 33. You said Washington Square West and this is Washington Square West," the driver said, without turning around.

"But it can't be," said Patti, rummaging in her bag for money and handing it to the driver as we got out of the cab and stood on the sidewalk with our belongings heaped around us. I looked over Patti's shoulder at the scrap of paper with the name and address written on it.

"There—you knew it all along," I said, kicking my suitcase away from the curb. "You knew his name—what's-his-name's. See—it's right there and you had it all along. Roger Coleman and . . ."

"Well, what if I did? I don't see what difference it makes. It simply doesn't matter." And Patti picked up her suitcase and started for the door.

"But it does," I said, my voice coming out louder than I had planned. "It does. It does."

"Sure, kid. It matters a lot. Don't let them tell you any different," said a boy who seemed to come out of nowhere, jumping over the sleeping bag and continuing on his way. At the corner he stopped and turned around, calling back to me, "It matters, kid. Just you remember that." And he was gone, running through the traffic and disappearing into the park across the street.

My face burned and I grabbed my stuff, bumping my way into the lobby in time to hear the tag end of Patti's conversation on the phone at the desk.

"Yes, Roger, that's right. You know—from Baltimore —and Henley, too. She's my daughter. That's right, and you said come and we came and we're in the lobby and we're coming up. Oh, just until we get a place of our own. Like you said, and Margey said . . ."

And all of a sudden that wonderful feeling I had had on the train—that maybe everything was going to be okay— started to seep away, like air out of an inner tube. I wanted to grab hold of something. "He didn't know we were coming, did he? I don't think he even knew who we were. I could tell. I heard you."

"Don't be ridiculous," said Patti, holding the elevator

door open. "How would you know anyway, what with standing out on the sidewalk and giving a speech. Of course he knew. He's thrilled. Maybe I just woke him up, is all. But a law school, for God's sake."

"Ye gods, Roger. A law school. You didn't say you lived in a law school," called Patti to the man standing in the open doorway at the end of the hall.

"I don't live in a law school. Even the classrooms look better than this. This is a dorm—NYU's finest," said Roger what's-his-name, nodding to me and leading the way into the living room. I tried to remember what he had looked like wrapped in a blanket, sleeping on our living-room floor.

"But you never said anything about school the other night. You and Margey . . ." Patti stepped over our belongings, which suddenly seemed to fill the room. She paced back and forth between the black plastic settee, which looked like all the others in the principal's office of every school I'd ever gone to, and the desk cluttered with books and notebooks and dirty coffee cups. "Where is she, anyway? Margey, I mean," said Patti, sidling past a table and a couple of straight-back chairs.

"At work, but she should be home any time now. Margey's a nurse over at St. Vincent's, and when she's working days, she usually gets home about now."

"A nurse—and a law student. But I thought . . . you said . . . well, it's not the way you made it out to be."

Roger shoved the chair into the desk and moved the floor lamp to the corner, as if by rearranging things he could push back the walls, make the room larger. I'd gladly have left and given them my space, but there wasn't anyplace to go. Besides, somebody had to watch out for Patti. He pushed the settee thump up against the wall and said, "Oh, you mean the other night in Baltimore. That was party talk—strictly party talk. A kind of fling, just after exams, and Margey had a few days off. I guess at times we all have to feel like the lilies of the field—that we spin not, neither do we toil. Only it doesn't work that way at all. This nurse and this law student spin and toil plenty." He began gathering books and papers into a pile on the top of his desk.

"But I don't understand. The other night at my place you and Margey and I seemed so—so all of a kind, I guess you'd say."

I hated the pleading sound in Patti's voice.

"And yesterday morning, when I came home early from work and woke you up, you both said it was a terrific idea for me to come to New York. You do remember that, don't you?" she said, taking a step toward Roger. "You haven't forgotten how you said you'd help me find a job, and an apartment, and how we could stay with you until we found them and how we'd all be one big damn happy family."

I hated her anger even more.

"It isn't just all for myself, you know. It's for Henley. So she can have advantages. There's so much here. So much she has to have. That's why I brought her here. Why she wanted to come. Why I gave up a job and an apartment and . . ."

Patti paced from wall to wall, from door to window, crisscrossing the room in paths that got shorter and shorter until she stopped in the middle of the floor and only her eyes seemed to continue on.

For the moment I didn't care that that wasn't the way it had happened. I cared about the tight rising sound of my mother's voice; about Roger shuffling law books and looking at the floor while Patti stood there giving too much of ourselves away.

"Don't worry about it, Patti," said Roger, slamming a desk drawer. "It's fine. Okay? There's room for all of us—rubber walls, you know. It's just that I have to study. I'm going over to the library, but you make yourselves at home. Margey will be here soon. She'll be glad to see you."

After Roger left, I didn't want to look at Patti, but then I realized that she had already forgotten about him, anyway. She moved to the table by the window, saying, "Just look at that view—the World Trade Center right there. See, I told you it would be all right. And it'll be even better when we get a place of our own. I wish Margey would get here. I want to go outside. To walk around and see it all and show it all to you."

I watched as Patti moved to the door of the kitchen, which was just large enough for one person moving sideways, then on to the bedroom and the bathroom. "It's not much, is it?" she said, coming back to stand at the window. "Not at all the way I pictured it. Maybe we'll go out awhile. Leave Margey a note that we've come and gone—and that we'll be back."

five

The black plastic settee was shorter than I was and the seat slanted downward, so that no matter how I lay, I rolled into the crack. I tried putting my head on the straight chair at the end of the couch, but as the furniture inched apart, I felt I was slowly being decapitated. I got up, smoothed the sheet over the slippery plastic, turned myself around, and climbed back onto the couch—this time with my feet on the straight-back chair. That didn't work either. The sheet slipped out from under me, my face slapped against the seat, and I got a noseful of that musty plastic smell.

Propping myself up on one elbow, I looked around the shadowed room at the jumble of open suitcases and clothes draped over chairs, and at Patti asleep in the sleeping bag. I leaned over, trying to see past the window edge to the shape of the World Trade Center, then planted my hands on the floor and jerked the settee away from the wall and into the room, on a line with the window.

I had to go to the bathroom. I tried not to have to go. I told myself that it was all in my imagination, that if I didn't think about it, it would go away. The more I didn't think about it, the more it didn't go away. Holding my breath, I listened to the sound of voices from Roger and Margey's room, tried to think what I'd say if they called out to me. I wondered where the light switch was in the bathroom and what I'd do if the door stuck and I couldn't get out again and had to stay there until morning. And what if the toilet overflowed. I eased up out of my makeshift bed, taking giant steps across the living room, past the now silent bedroom door, and into the bathroom. The light switch sounded like a shot, and a cockroach ran across the sink. Margey's white panty hose dangling from the shower rod brushed against my face and towels and washrags and a peach-colored terry-cloth robe hung all around me. When I was finished, I took a deep breath and flushed the toilet, jamming my fingers into my ears and waiting for the rush of water and the clatter of pipes inside the walls to fade away. I ran back to bed.

By that time, I was wide awake.

The day seemed to jiggle inside my head: I felt the lickety-click of the train still trundling me along and put my hand down on the floor to stop the motion. Lickety-click. Lickety-click. Cars and taxis and buses crowded in on me: horns blew, elevator doors slammed shut, subways vibrated the sidewalks overhead. I closed my eyes and faces swirled against the insides of the lids. I opened my eyes and

46

the faces still swam at me: the taxi driver, Roger, the woman on the train, Margey, Patti, and the men on park benches and children in the street; the waitress in the restaurant, the man selling chestnuts on the corner, the juggler, and the woman feeding pigeons.

I tried to push my way through the lights and voices that streaked around me, to force my way back into yesterday. I closed my eyes and tried to see Mary Jane and Mrs. Goodman with her bakery bags, or Mr. Barber peering through his kitchen curtains. I tried to see the toad-ugly shape on the bedroom ceiling. But it was as if they never were.

The room seemed to spook around me. The floor lamp was suddenly an ostrich with its neck crooked at a funny angle. When I rolled on my back, the shadows on the walls quickly turned into tall and narrow buildings spiking up around me. I flopped over on my side, sending the chair away from the couch and humping my knees up beside my chest, and then I saw Margey's nurse shoes shining white against the shadows underneath the table and I latched on to those shoes, staring at them; concentrating; trying to stop the racing inside my stomach that felt as if maybe I was going to throw up. I hate to throw up.

Margey had come in from work just as we had been ready to go out. "Surprise," Patti called when Margey opened the door, and there was something in her voice, something raw and trusting all at the same time, that made me turn away and look down to the street below, watching a woman with a tiny black dog until they turned the corner and disappeared. More than anything, I didn't *want* Margey to be surprised, didn't want to feel the same astonishment I had felt in Roger as Patti and I had bumbled our way down the hall toward him.

"Bet you didn't think we'd come, but we did," Patti hurried on, catching me by the arm and pulling me around just as Margey had kicked off her shoes, sending them under the table. "I told you we'd come. That we could pick up at a moment's notice. We travel light. But all that's going to change, isn't it, Henley. Now that we're here. We're going to settle down. Oh, by the way, this is Henley— Henley, Margey."

"Hi, Henley," said Margey. "Well, it is a surprise. I mean, did you see Roger? I'll bet he was surprised—but glad to see you both. Let me just get out of this uniform and . . ."

Then I went back to stand at the window, leaning my head against the glass and looking down, wondering about the woman with her dog, trying not to hear the insistence in Patti's voice as she followed Margey into the bedroom.

After Margey changed into jeans, we went out, walking around Washington Square, past students and kids on bikes and old men slouched on park benches; past boys with radios slung over their shoulders, and children on swings, and an old woman with pigeons lined down her arms as though she were a statue. We stood under the arch watching the piano player and listening to him sing about "Poor Butterfly." I wondered how he got his piano there and how he got it home again and where home for him was anyway. Margey pointed out the law school, the library, and

Washington Mews and asked Patti when she planned to look for an apartment all in the same breath. We went down West Fourth Street and across Sixth Avenue to a seafood house, working our way through the carry-out shop in front to the back dining room, where candles flickered on the tables and the knots of conversation were low and intense.

"See, Henley, didn't I tell you how it would be?" Patti said, her voice peaking above the other voices in the room. "She didn't want to come. Didn't think you and Roger really wanted us. I tried to explain how you all stayed with us . . . how we're here now."

I dug the tines of my fork into the place mat—right in the middle of the picture of a bluefish—and felt embarrassed for my mother, angry at myself for feeling embarrassed, and angry at Patti for making me feel that way. It got so complicated I could feel things pulling inside my head. I wondered how Patti could let her own voice just glide along, not hearing the held-back tone as Margey said, "Apartments aren't easy to come by—with rent control and all that. People tend to hang on to what they've got. As soon as we get back, we'll check the paper. And for jobs, too."

"My God, Margey, I'll get a job and an apartment." I guess Patti had heard what Margey was saying, after all. Her voice was sharp, until she suddenly changed it, as though she were changing the speed on a stereo. She went on, slowly and carefully. "We won't stay long. I promise you that. And we won't be in the way a bit, will we, Henny-penny?" She kicked me under the table, rolling her eyes toward Margey, who was studying the menu. Right away I had the awful feeling that it didn't matter to Patti what Margey wanted at all.

"But not tomorrow," Patti said. "That's for Henley and me. A perfect day. I'm going to give her one perfect day."

"One perfect day." I held on to that phrase, carrying it with me through the rest of dinner and afterwards as we walked down Seventh Avenue and across Bleecker Street and back up to the apartment. I still held on to those words, like a kind of charm, as I fished around with my feet and tried to reattach the chair to the rest of that awful plastic lumped-up bed, staring at Margey's white shoes underneath the table.

"One perfect day . . . one perfect day . . ."

It seemed that I had scarcely gotten to sleep when Roger stumbled against the end of the couch, spilling coffee and cursing loudly. He went into the bedroom and for a minute I thought about trying to listen; but instead gave up and shrugged my way back into sleep again. From somewhere far away I saw Margey moving through the room, rummaging for her shoes, picking up her shoulder bag. I heard the sound of the door and the distant rumbling of the elevator. I slid into sleep and then out again as Roger stopped to gather his books and stepped over Patti in the sleeping bag and went out the door. I heard him call to someone and run down the hall, heard the elevator door again.

The next time I woke, the room was filled with sunlight. The sheet was scrunched down in the crack and I felt hot and sticky on the plastic seat. There was a little pool of spit underneath my face, and the inside of my mouth tasted like galoshes—or the way I think galoshes would taste. I do that sometimes, think about words that way. Take boots— they could have a leathery okay taste. Mine was definitely a galoshes mouth. I eased over on my back and squinted at the window where a fat brown pigeon stood on the sill staring in at me.

"Hey, Patti," I called. "You know what I think? I think we shouldn't be here. I mean, I don't think they want us here. Roger and Margey—"

"My God, don't start," said Patti, sitting up and peeling her T-shirt up over her head and tossing it across the room. "At least you had a bed. I didn't sleep a wink. Tonight you get the sleeping bag. Come on—get up. There's so much for us to do. So much to see."

"Put something on," I said, untangling the sheet from under the couch. "Somebody might come. Roger, or anybody."

Patti stood in front of the window stretching slowly, reaching upward. Sideways. Letting the sun warm her body. She rapped on the glass until the pigeon hiked up its feathers like some funny old lady gathering her skirts, and flew away. Then she swung around to face me. "I don't hear you nagging me. Don't hear you at all. Not today. Come on, lazybones. We're going out."

We got the bus on the corner of Sixth Avenue and Eighth Street, and sat on the long seat behind the driver, slipping and sliding as the bus lurched its way uptown. I stared out the window across from me at stores and delicatessens and office buildings; at the wholesale florists

51

with the potted plants jumbled out onto the sidewalk, and the racks of clothes going along as if on their own; at people hurrying past us while the bus hung suspended in traffic, and at those same people left behind when the bus suddenly lunged forward. I craned my neck to see out the window in back of me, catching a trace of spring through the open window, spring mixed with exhaust fumes, and turned to watch a man pushing a typewriter table down the aisle of the bus. I looked over the shoulder of the man next to me as he read a newspaper printed in what Patti said was Yiddish, and watched a woman take a jelly doughnut out of her briefcase and eat it.

I swung around to face Patti, suddenly needing to know she was there. For a minute it was as if she knew what I needed. She squeezed my hand and said, "We'll go to the park first, and then maybe the zoo and the museum."

"But how do you know—where, I mean?" I said, catching myself as the bus stopped short.

"Because I've been here before. I told you—when I was little—and then when I was in college."

"But what if the bus turns. What if . . ."

"What if, what if, what if, what if . . ." Patti chattered back at me. "Come on, 'What if,' it's time to get off. There's Central Park over there."

I followed behind Patti, losing her for a moment in the scramble to get off the bus, then darting through a crowd of boys to find her. "Wait up."

"Catch up," said Patti, walking faster. "Keep up," she called back over her shoulder as she ducked around a doorman with gold braid on his coat. I raced along behind her, trying to keep her in view, all the while wondering what would happen if I lost sight of her. We went around a corner and Patti stopped, looking at the building to her right and waiting for me. "The Plaza Hotel," she whispered in a voice that sounded as if she had just discovered the pot of gold at the end of the rainbow. She caught my arm and steered me up the steps. "I thought it was here. Elegant— and *so* chic. Come on."

"No—don't," I said, pulling back. "Don't go in there." One thing I knew was that I didn't want to go into the Plaza Hotel.

"Don't be silly," said Patti, sailing through the door with her head up. "Act as if you belong here and you will. Look over there. In the afternoon there's tea—and someone playing the violin. We'll come someday."

Patti whirled us through the lobby and out the side door and across the street, where the horse-drawn carriages were lined along the curb. I reached out, touching the muzzle of the first horse in line, and for a minute I could almost feel myself riding in a carriage, sitting up straight next to Patti, bowing and smiling. I wanted to do it and didn't want to do it, and didn't want Patti to know I was even thinking about it. I lowered my head and hurried past, moving out in front of her, away from any idea she might suddenly have of taking a carriage ride, right out in public with all of New York looking on.

We went into the park, stepping around pigeons and children in strollers; stopping to get hot dogs and sodas; sitting on a bench and trying not to notice the weirdo swathed in mufflers who was predicting that potato bugs would one day take over the subway system as he waved his half-eaten pretzel at us.

After lunch we went to the zoo. We went past the pony carts and down the steps to the sea lions, and then on around the monkeys and lions and elephants. We ate peanuts and ice-cream bars, following the little signs to the carrousel.

"I'm going to ride," said Patti, shoving the money in the window cage at the ticket seller and handing two tickets to me. And then, before I even had time to protest, the gong sounded and we were on horses and going around and around and up and down. I closed my eyes and felt as though I could keep on riding forever.

But not with Patti around. "I told you how it would be," she said, grabbing hold of me and pulling me off the horse and away from the carrousel, out onto the path. "Somewhere there's a lake—and boats—and old men playing checkers. Come on—I want to show you Fifth Avenue."

"It's too much," I said, following Patti into the bookstore at the museum. "It's too much and it goes so fast that I can't see anything. It's all a blur." I felt I wanted to kick at things.

"Good God," said Patti, stopping and pushing her hair away from her face. "Here we are in the Metropolitan Museum of Art and you're talking about a blur."

And blur or no blur, I was suddenly ravenously hungry. "I'm hungry," I said, staring down at my tennis shoes and grinding one against the other.

"Hungry? Hungry?" And for a moment I didn't know

which way Patti's mood was going to go. Then she said, "Me too," and started to laugh. "What'll it be? Tea at the Plaza? Or here at the cafeteria by the pool, all bunched around with naked statues peeing in the water."

"Pat—ti . . ."

"Pat—ti what?"

"Why can't you . . ."

"Why can't I what?"

"Be like other mothers," I said all in a rush. "Sometimes. Some times."

"Okay—okay. It's other-mothers you want," said Patti, mincing around a display table with her shoulder bag hooked over her arm. "I'm other-mothers going to a committee meeting. Other-mothers playing bridge at the country club. Other-mothers-other-mothers-other-mothers . . ." I heard Patti's voice, which had been singsong, stretch to a taut flat line.

"I was just kidding," I said quickly. "It was a joke. Come on, please. Let's go." I wasn't hungry anymore.

"Okay, Miss Priss, I'll stop," said Patti, taking one final swing around the table. "Here, buy some postcards. Whatever you want. I want to find one to send to Angel. Postcards and then we'll go."

I moved up and down the rack of cards, looking for something for Mary Jane and for Mrs. Goodman. I picked up a picture of a naked statue without arms and thought I'd send it to Mr. Barber the pervert and how it wasn't the arms he was interested in anyway. Then I put it back and chose one card—for me—because I liked it. I paid the cashier and went out to sit in the Great Hall, studying

55

The Unicorn in Captivity, running my finger over the glossy smoothness of the card—white and green and red and brown.

I trailed along behind Patti down all the steps of the Metropolitan Museum of Art; down Fifth Avenue along the outside of the park; across the street and past the Hotel Pierre. Then I started to run—if you can call it running—in and out of crowds and around people until we were side by side and I wasn't following along behind her anymore. She pushed me through a door, coming in after me, saying, "Choose something. Anything you want."

"But, Patti, it's a toy store, and I'm too old for toys."

Patti draped her arms around the neck of a four-foot-high camel and did a kind of dance. "But, Henley, let me tell you something—it's not *any* toy store—it's *the* toy store —the ultimate. The best. And I always said when I had a kid I was going to buy her something at F. A. O. Schwarz. I even sent for a catalogue once, only your father and his parents laughed and poked at me. They wanted to know what was wrong with J. C. Penney, for God's sake. J. C. Penney, I ask you."

Patti propelled me past the stuffed animals, on through the dolls and games. We went up the stairs to dollhouses and Erector Sets and toy typewriters that clicked and little pianos that tinkled and trains that ran on tracks above our heads. We went back down again, this time by elevator.

"Well, how about it? What do you want?"

"But, Patti—I mean, well, it's expensive here. So much money and I don't need anything . . . don't want anything."

56

"It's like the English pram I wanted you to have, only I guess it's too late for that now," said Patti, holding a stuffed monkey out at arm's length. "Choose something. Anything. Whatever. Choose it all." And Patti seemed to be going round and round like the wind-up bear going in circles on the counter in front of us.

I looked around for the smallest thing I could find and pointed to a tiny stuffed bear, smaller than my hand, on the glass shelf behind the counter.

"We'll have a bear," said Patti grandly to the saleswoman. "The one there, on the shelf."

The woman put the toy bear in a box and stuffed it all around with tissue paper, lovingly and carefully and very slowly. I moved down the counter, sliding away from Patti, hoping the woman wouldn't think the bear was for me.

"Thirty-five dollars, plus tax," the saleswoman said in a voice that sounded like heavy cream. I almost choked—and got that awful cold-all-over feeling.

"Patti, no. All that money." I said, pulling at her arm. "Stop. Put it back. I only picked it because it was the littlest thing there and I didn't think it would cost much. Hardly anything at all. Because you said I had to choose something. Because you wanted me to have something."

Patti handed the money over as if she bought thirty-five-dollar bears every day of the week. She took the package and headed for the door. "It's my money," she said when we were outside. "And I can do what I want with it and what I wanted to do was to buy something at F. A. O. Schwarz and I did. Take it."

I caught the bag she tossed at me, and my voice—my

thank you—was lifted and blown away somewhere above our heads.

"Let's go home—to Margey's place," I said as we pushed open the heavy doors of St. Patrick's Cathedral and went outside, away from the smell of wax, incense, and cool, cool air. "I'm tired. And my feet hurt. I don't want to go anyplace else."

"But just over there is Saks Fifth Avenue, then there's Rockefeller Center, where they ice-skate in winter."

"It's not winter," I said, sitting down on the step, sticking my legs out in front of me, and picking at the end of the white paper bag until it was worn soft. Not caring if I ever saw Rockefeller Center.

"Here, give me that thing," said Patti, taking the Schwarz bag and putting it under her arm as she moved restlessly from one step to another. I watched Patti as she stood looking down Fifth Avenue, and thought that she wasn't so much having fun as wanting to have fun. Part of me wanted to get up, to let Patti take me up and down curbs, across streets and through revolving doors; zigzagging between cars and buses and taxi cabs. But my feet hurt and there was a burning place between my shoulder blades. I didn't move.

We stayed that way for a minute: Patti so obviously ready to go anywhere; and me content to just sit there with the pigeons on the steps of St. Patrick's Cathedral.

After a while she put her hand out and said, "Okay. We'll get a bus."

We got off just as the bus turned onto Eighth Street and it wasn't until we were cutting through the park that Patti stopped and swung around. "Oh no," she said. "The bag. We left the bag on the bus."

I thought of the little bear, no larger than my hand, still packed in tissue paper, being trundled off on that ugly bus.

So much for a perfect day.

six

"We went ahead and ate," said Margey, looking up from the table as Patti and I came into the apartment, and from the look on her face you'd have thought she had eaten worms. "Because we didn't know what your plans were, what you were going to do. Here," she said, pushing at a plate in the middle of the table. "There's tuna left. And some potato chips in a bag in the kitchen. Pull up a chair." Margey inched her way slightly toward the window.

"One of you can sit here," said Roger, getting up and clearing his place. "I've got to go to the library. There are extra plates in the kitchen."

I looked around the room at the jumble of open suitcases, the knapsack, my basket tilting into the front of the desk, and suddenly felt as extra as the plates. Reaching to close Patti's suitcase, I tried to kick the sleeping bag under the couch.

"Don't worry about us," said Patti, flopping down on a chair—which clearly meant *she* wasn't worrying. "We're going out. We want to eat Italian tonight. But afterwards I'll bring Henley back and drop her off and maybe the three of us can go someplace. Do something. Cut loose."

"Better count us out," said Margey, pushing her chair away from the table. "This is my night to do the laundry, and I want to get to bed early."

"It's a weeknight—Margey has to be at work before seven," said Roger. "But maybe over the weekend we could do something."

His words were almost lost in the clatter of dishes as Margey started to clear the table, glaring and prickling all over like an angry porcupine. Looking around the room, I guess I could see what she was upset about. I mean, we were so *there.* But on the other hand it was *us* she was glaring and prickling at and that made me feel really peculiar. I could see why Margey was mad, then was mad at her for being mad at us. Roger mumbled and shrugged, looking at no one in particular, and went out with his arms full of books, letting the door slam shut behind him.

For a moment there was silence, like the gap between the end of one television show and the beginning of another.

Suddenly the apartment was crowded with the whirl-wind of Margey moving back and forth. I could feel the air stirring in the corners as I saw her pull a laundry basket out of the closet and come out of the bedroom with an armload of towels and jeans and shirts, with underwear and socks dangling from the pile. She stepped over Patti's stretched-out feet and went in and out of the kitchen, adding

61

a box of Tide to the mound of clothes. She shook her wallet onto the table, sliding the quarters for the washer and dryer into her hand and leaving the nickels and pennies and dimes spread where they fell.

It was as though the non-conversation was getting louder. I stared at Patti, willing her to stop filing her nails, to say something, to stop Margey as she huffed her way around the room. But Patti just kept acting as if she didn't notice a thing, holding her fingers out in front of her, then turning her hand, crooking her fingers toward her and keeping them that way until Margey stood at the apartment door and called back over her shoulder, "The paper's there on the desk. Help-wanted is in the back."

"This is the way we wash the clothes, wash the clothes, wash the clothes. This is the way we wash the clothes, all on a Monday morning," sang Patti as she grabbed me by the hands and swung me around the room. "Except it isn't Monday, it's Wednesday and I'm starving. Come on, let's get out of here."

The words lumped up inside me almost in spite of myself. Words about how we shouldn't have come and shouldn't be here and how we were in the way and no wonder Margey was mad. But Patti had me by the hands and was spinning me around and I wanted to keep on spinning. "This is the way we eat Italian, all on a Wednesday evening," sang Patti, going faster and faster, until the clothes and the suitcases and the clutter of furniture dissolved into a kind of streak that trailed behind us, and I was hanging on for dear life.

"Tomorrow we'll find a place of our own," said Patti, turning over on the couch. "Someplace with real beds and where we don't have to whisper and where people don't get up in the middle of the night to go to work."

"Shhhh," I said from my place in the sleeping bag on the floor. "They'll hear you."

"Or study all the time." The couch creaked as Patti turned from one side to the other. "Where we can have fun."

"How about a job? You should get a job first."

"I will get a job," said Patti, swinging her legs around and sitting up. "Just you wait and see. A wonderful job, but first . . ."

"A job first," I said, staring at the pattern on the ceiling made by the lights outside. "A job, so we'll know about money. About what we have."

I stopped talking and let out a deep sigh and felt as though I had been carrying something that was heavy and was looking for a place to put it down.

"Just for once, trust me," Patti said. "Because I have a feeling that this is where we're supposed to be. This time it's going to be different. Okay?"

"I liked it where we were. And the place before that. Why didn't we bring a pillow?" I said, thumping over on my side and feeling the floor poking into my bones, or the bones into the floor. So much for the sleeping bag.

"Use your arm," said Patti, going to stand by the window. "Anyway, they were dull—those other places. Dull and stick-in-the-muddish."

"But there were friends there. Mary Jane—and before that there was Paula—and before that . . ."

"Before that, nothing," said Patti, her voice cracking

out of a whisper. "My God, there are kids everyplace. Probably in this very building or the one next door or in the park."

"Shhhh," I said, sitting up. "Anyway, we're not going to *be* here all that long even if there were kids—even if . . ."

"Now it's 'even if,' " said Patti, coming over and sitting on the floor next to the sleeping bag. " 'Even if'—'What if' —'But, Patti.' Look, sweetie, I guess for a few days you'll just have to put up with me. And Margey. And Roger. And the old lady at the switchboard. After all, I brought you here. I gave up my job and everything so you could have advantages."

Suddenly it occurred to me that whenever Patti wanted me to do something I didn't want to do—or something that she especially did want to do—she called it an advantage. As if that was supposed to make it all okay. The only trouble is, there are advantages that are. And advantages that aren't.

I had to shake myself and say very quickly, "No, it wasn't like that. You *know* it wasn't like that." Then I held my breath, waiting for her anger. For her insistence.

When Patti finally spoke, I could hardly hear her. "I don't think how we got here matters as much as the fact that we *are* here. It's just that there's so much out there. So much for both of us," said Patti, getting up on her knees. "There's a song the mock turtle sang: '. . . turn not pale, beloved snail, but come and join the dance.' " And Patti swayed from side to side. " 'Will you, won't you, will you, won't you, will you join the dance?' "

"I remember," I said, wrapping my arms around my knees.

64

"From *Alice in Wonderland*," said Patti, leaning closer to me. "Will you, won't you, will you, won't you . . . It's just that we have to get it all, Henny-penny. See it all and do it all and store it away."

"But, Patti . . ." And I wanted to tell her it would be easier to join the dance if we could stay somewhere long enough to learn the steps. But she was going on. "Because I know what you can do—have seen the things you write. Remember the teacher in that last school who called me in to show me your stories."

"School before last," I said, watching Patti's face as it loomed closer and closer.

"And before that, on my own. The things you wrote at home. Things you used to show me. There's something special there, but it's the kind of gift that's going to make you give something back. You have to be ready for it, Henny-penny. To join the dance. I guess I'm not right about very many things—but I know I'm right about that."

And for a long time things were quiet between us. Then I lay down, stretching out flat and putting my hand up to my face as if trying to hold on to the cool tracings Patti's fingers had made against my cheek before she had turned and gone back to the couch.

I kept thinking about this Patti and the things she had said; and about the other Patti, who so much of the time seemed to be wearing me away. And about what would happen when there wasn't anything left, and about how I sometimes saw myself as a snake running out of skins.

I thought about all this as if I should be able to make sense of it—only I couldn't. Thought about it long after Patti had gone to sleep.

65

"A job," said Patti, who was standing at the window brushing her hair when I woke up. "Today I'm going to find a job. And an apartment. It's not exactly the Welcome Wagon around here."

"Can I come with you?" I asked, getting up off the floor and reaching for my clothes.

"No."

"What'll I do then?"

"Do? Do? Do whatever you want. Poke around here. Go to the park, ride a bus, go somewhere to eat, walk up Fifth Avenue, or count the pigeons." Patti stepped over the sleeping bag and swung around. "There—do I look sensible? And proper?"

"I can see through that blouse," I said.

"Oh, damn," said Patti, ripping off the blouse and throwing it on the floor. "Find me something suitable, then. Something sturdy and serviceable and—and chaste, for crying out loud."

After Patti had gone, I picked up her blouse and crawled under the table to find the missing buttons. I took off my pajama top and slipped into the blouse, letting the soft white cloth whisper around my body, smelling the faint Patti-smell. Then I wandered into the bedroom looking for a mirror and stood posing behind the door, one hand on my hip, the other holding my hair up on top of my head.

"Yes," I said out loud. "I've come about the job—the one in the *Times*. Experience? Oh yes, lots of experience. Tons. I've done *everything*. But it's like this, I have this kid and she wants to be someplace and stay there. And I promised her that this time we would. You see, it's important to her." All of a sudden, when I heard those words coming from the person looking back out of the mirror, I knew that they had nothing to do with Patti at all. They were all mine. I stuffed my fist up to my mouth as if I could cram them back where they came from, and turned away from the mirror and started pulling at the blouse. Just the way the real Patti had done.

I grabbed my clothes and went to take a shower, turning the water on full force and rubbing shampoo into my hair. I let the soap run down into my eyes, not caring how much it stung. I choked and spit and thought for a minute that I was going to drown right there in the shower at old what's-his-name's apartment. Then I turned and let the water beat down against my back and said, "H, my name is Henley, and I come from Henlopen . . ." as loud as I could.

Afterwards I hung up the towels in the bathroom, cleaned the tub and made the bed, rolled the sleeping bag as tight as I could, shoving it into a closet along with the covers from the black plastic settee. I washed the dishes, stacked them in the cupboard, and watered the plants.

Then I ran out of things to do. I tried to read, but I wasn't in the mood. I opened my journal, turned to a clean page, and sat staring down at it. After a while I slammed the notebook, shoved it under the cushion on the couch, and got up and went out.

Outside, I found an empty bench near the west side of the park, away from the old men sleeping and spitting and talking in their whiny voices and drinking out of bottles wrapped in brown paper bags. I was careful to sit so that I could see the door of the apartment house; as if I were attached to it by a long thin wire. The sun was warm and the street noises had a faraway sound as though they were a background for the closer sounds of skates and radios and barking dogs.

All of a sudden I heard the wail of a siren as it got closer, peaked, and faded out again. I clenched the slats of the bench and thought about fire engines and ambulances and police cars with blinking lights. I wondered where Patti was. And the wondering threatened to swallow me up. I tried to summon up the picture of Patti in her sensible blouse and skirt going from office to office, in and out of revolving doors.

The echo of that siren made me close my eyes and see, somewhere, a street with Patti crumpled down on it, cars held at bay, strangers moving past, scarcely looking down, policemen and . . .

Opening my eyes, I tried to shake off the terrible coldness that crept up around me. I stared at a boy walking a basset hound and at an old woman in a purple muumuu rummaging through a wire trash basket, and I wanted to run up to them and shake them and have them know I was there. I wanted to hear the sound of my own voice.

"H, my name is Henley, and I come from Henlopen, and I eat hen's eggs . . ." I said very softly under my breath. "And Patti's out there somewhere, and if anything happened to her, I'd never know, because nobody'd know she belonged here—or to me."

I cleared my throat and swallowed hard, but the thoughts kept pushing at me. Then I thought of something else: how long would Roger and Margey keep me there and where would they send me when they wouldn't keep me anymore. I felt a sudden lump in my throat for Patti lying crumpled and hurt and a victim of amnesia, and for myself drifting and bobbling along with no place to go, while Margey stepped over the offending sleeping bag and Roger sighed and complained about having to go to the library to study.

Then I felt really dumb for thinking all those things, as if I were in the middle of a soap opera, and remembered how Patti said I sometimes let my imagination run wild. But it kept right on running. It was suddenly very important that I plan it all out: what I would do, where I would go.

Maybe back to Baltimore. Maybe to Angel or to Mrs. Goodman down the block or to Mary Jane's, only her mother had enough kids already. The palms of my hands began to sweat and I wiped them down the sides of my jeans. "There's always Eric," I thought, but then I remembered how Eric used to stop talking when I was around. How he and Patti had a fight late one night and Eric had left, slamming the door, and we hadn't seen him again. The pain inside my stomach dug deeper and deeper.

"Aunt Mercy." I said the words out loud and there was an okayness about them. "I'll go to Aunt Mercy," I thought, sitting up straighter and sighing deeply. "Aunt Mercy—Dr. Mercedes somebody or other . . . in . . ." I realized that I didn't know any more about Aunt Mercy than Patti had parceled out in the once-upon-a-time stories she had told. Before now, I had never had to know.

The bench shook beneath me. There was a great flopping and flouncing and swirling of purple as the old woman in the muumuu settled down beside me. She leaned into me, her breath coming in sour spurts, as she said, "Here by yourself, missy? Spending the day alone? I've come to keep you company."

I pulled back sharply, then caught myself, not wanting to hurt her feelings—but not wanting to smell her, either—and inched my way along the bench. "No. I'm waiting for my mother. She's off looking for a job, but she'll be back after a while."

"A job?" the woman said, repeating the word as though I had spoken in a foreign language. Then she leaned forward, rummaging in her plastic shopping bag and pulling out a paper bag tightened around the shape of a bottle.

"Coffee," she said after a long swallow. "I'd offer it around except I have a cold. Wouldn't want you to catch a cold." She took another swallow and shoved the bottle down into the bag. "My name is Gloria, by the way.

"This is the best park in New York," the woman went on. "And I've tried them all. Used to take the subway up to Fort Tryon Park—and to Central Park. Now I mostly stay around here. Then there's Gramercy Park—snooty, though, if you want to know—and then there's . . ."

"We went to Central Park yesterday," I said, inching farther down the bench. "Patti and I." I heard a soft hissing noise and turned to see Gloria sound asleep, with her head dropped down on her chest, her mouth puckering in and out with every breath.

70

For a while I sat listening to the snuffling sound of the old woman's breathing and watching two pigeons fighting over a chunk of Cracker Jack lying on the ground. After a bit I stood up, stepping around the pigeons so as not to start them fluttering, and went along the street by the side of the park. Every few steps, I turned to see my way back, and then moved forward as though I were playing out the invisible wire that held me to the apartment house.

Turning the corner onto Eighth Street, I stood still, memorizing the location of the ice-cream parlor on one corner and the delicatessen across the street. Then, taking a big gulp, I started up one side of the street. I ate pizza at a stand-up counter and washed it down with orange juice. I poked at T-shirts hanging on a sidewalk rack and listened to a blind man playing an accordion and looked at postcards and posters and spiral notebooks with the Beatles on the covers. When I got to Fifth Avenue, I crossed Eighth Street and started down the other side: past a health-food store with bunches of herbs drying in the window, and a shoemaker, and a Chinese laundry. In the cookie store I stood leaning on the counter until it was my turn, then ordered a pound of chocolate-chip cookies.

When I got back to the corner, the one thing I really wanted to do was to turn and hurry back to the park, to the shadow of the apartment building, but I forced myself to continue down to Sixth Avenue. Heading back up Eighth Street, I passed a record store with the music playing out onto the sidewalk. I stopped in front of a bookstore and ran my fingers along the spines of the paperback books outside. Then suddenly it was as if I had been away long enough. I began to run, dodging people and dogs on leashes and fire hydrants and plastic bags of garbage, feeling somehow that I had to get back to my place in the park. So that Patti would come home all right.

Once inside the park, I stood for a minute looking across at Gloria, who still sat with her head lolling forward on her chest as if she hadn't moved. Right away I started making a story about her, shaping a past around her and decking her out in might-have-beens. I thought how she was really an exiled Russian princess, maybe even the one I'd seen the television show about—Anastasia herself. And how, all the time people had been wondering about her, she was right here sitting on a bench in Washington Square, under the name of Gloria. And I was the only one who knew. I looked at her again and suddenly I didn't want to make a story about her anymore. Sitting there, she just looked terribly alone. I didn't know what else to do, so I sat down on the end of the bench and put the bag of cookies there between us.

"And then there's Riverside Park," Gloria said, sliding along the bench toward me and reaching her hand into the bag for a cookie. "And Battery Park." She reached for another cookie, shoving it into her mouth. "I was telling you about them before I dozed off for a minute there."

After a few minutes Gloria scratched her head and said, "Morningside Park." And reached for another cookie.

We sat in silence for a while. Then I heard, "East River Park," as the woman rooted in the bag.

"Bryant Park." Reach went her hand.

"And Union Square."

"I love parks," she said, pulling the bottle out of her

shopping bag and taking a gurgling swallow. "Almost as much as I love cookies."

We sat together on the bench through all that long, comfortable afternoon, watching pigeons and joggers and sunlight and shadows on the grass. I saw the white-paper cookie bag getting emptier and emptier as Gloria named her way through the parks of New York City.

seven

I've never been able to figure out whether we left New York because I told Patti we had to, or whether she had already decided we were going to leave before I said what I did, so that it didn't really matter. The way it doesn't matter if the wind blows the paper cup away after the soda is gone and you were getting ready to toss it anyway.

That was the thing about Patti.

I just never knew.

It was the day after I had met Gloria in the park, and Patti and I were sitting at the table picking at chocolate doughnuts and at a conversation.

"There I was, out looking for a job, and there you were, eating cookies with a wino in the park," she said, playing with her mug until the coffee sloshed out onto the table.

"She wasn't a wino and her name was Gloria and she

74

was okay—nice, sort of, and lonely. Besides, I was getting experiences—like you said. You said, 'Go out and find something to do.' You said . . ."

"Said what?" said Patti. "Said. Said. Said. I'm all the time being boxed in with 'saids.' 'Said this . . .' 'Said that . . .' Margey said, 'Find a job . . .' And Roger said, 'Find another place to stay . . . It's not fair to Margey, having people sleeping in the living room, as hard as she works.' "

"They really said that?" I mean, I knew all along that that's the way it felt in the apartment. But I didn't know they'd come right out and said it. Especially old what's-his-name Roger.

"Yes, they did, too. They said it yesterday when they sent you out for rolls. That's class, sending you to Balducci's so they could lecture me. 'For your own good,' they said. Just like your father said, 'Settle down . . . give it a chance.' And my mother said, 'Be a good girl, Patti.' "

It was as if I had run out into traffic like some kind of crazy crossing guard with my hands up to hold back the cars and buses and trucks that were hurtling toward me in the form of Patti's words.

"*Stop.*" I said. "Can't you see that we have to get out of here. We shouldn't be here at all. Why can't you see that? And now you tell me that they actually said what they said and . . ." Even while I was talking, I had dragged my suitcase up off the floor and plunked it down on the settee and was stuffing clothes inside. "We have to go. The only way we could stay would be if you had a job and we could get a place of our own."

"You know damn well I didn't get a job. You know what they said. 'We're not hiring at the moment. Job

75

experience is spotty. Leave a résumé. We'll be in touch.' Then there was the prize: 'Have you thought of the typing pool?' Oh, my God, the typing pool."

I put Patti's suitcase on the table, saying, "We'll go back to Baltimore," and started gathering up her shirts and bras and shoes and shoving them in any which way. All the while, I was thinking about our old apartment and wondering if we could get it back, and about *Blue Boy* on the wall, and Mary Jane and our aquarium play, and Mr. Barber the pervert. The next thing I knew, Patti was right in there shoving things into the suitcase and saying in a drifting kind of voice, "Yes—we'll go back to Baltimore. To Angel's to get our things and the car and maybe to call Eric. Maybe to work something out. I have it all figured out—I'll go back to the ad agency and tell them that I have to have a chance, that I had this wonderful opportunity in New York but that I turned it down."

The thing was, I think she really believed it.

Out on the street, I whistled for a cab, and the amazing thing was that a real whistle came out. All those times I had tried, putting two fingers in my mouth and pursing my lips till I almost choked. Nothing. But this time I whistled the most glorious piercing whistle that seemed to split the air.

And a cab stopped.

Maybe it was an omen.

I looked out of the cab window at the streets that were as familiar as if I had known them for a long, long time. We passed the park and I looked over my shoulder, to see if Gloria was on the bench. She wasn't. We went by students running to catch up to other students; men cleaning the sidewalks with hoses; past the fish house and the fruit vendor and the ice-cream parlor. I didn't want to look anymore. Instead, I stared at the back of the driver's head, his neck bristled and hunched down inside his yellow jacket. I studied the picture of his face and memorized his name—Nicholas Fazenhiemer—and tried to put him all together front to back. "Nicholas Fazenhiemer—Nicholas Fazenhiemer," I rolled the name around inside my head and found it picking up bits and pieces of a story the way a snowball picks up layers of snow and grows and grows.

"Nicholas Fazenhiemer," I thought. "And his wife Magdalena. Nicholas and Magdalena Fazenhiemer. And they live in an apartment over an Italian bakery, so there are always plenty of cannolis for the Fazenhiemer twins, only Magdalena doesn't work in the bakery, because she's a ballerina, and every night she goes off to dance and Nicholas Fazenhiemer stays at home with the twins and helps them with their homework and practices piano, because someday he's going to play at Carnegie Hall. On Friday nights he and the twins, who are girls, go to the ballet and sit in the balcony and watch Magdalena dance and . . ."

Nicholas Fazenhiemer slammed on his brakes. I lurched forward and caught hold of Patti. Together we flopped back against the seat. I closed my eyes and tried to force myself back into being one of the Fazenhiemer twins (the one with the crippled leg). She was at the ballet, watching her mother dance. It was *Swan Lake* and the house lights had dimmed: the conductor had taken the podium.

Horns blew and Nicholas Fazenhiemer shook his fist out the window. I blinked my eyes and sighed. I picked up my basket, reaching for my notebook to write down bits of the story before they got away.

"It's gone," I said, pulling my pajamas and the wooden box and the postcard of *The Unicorn in Captivity* out of the basket. "My journal's not here."

"Maybe it's in the suitcase," said Patti. "You probably packed it there, the way you were shoveling things away."

"I didn't. I know for sure, because I thought about it, but I knew I wanted it in the basket in case I wanted it for the train. It was under the seat of the black plastic couch and I . . . ." Then I stopped, feeling my face turn hot and creeping red. "And . . . and I left it there."

"Don't worry," said Patti, rooting in her wallet for money. "If she ever finds it, Margey will use the unused pages for making lists. She's definitely a list-maker: grocery lists and laundry lists: things to do and books to read. A real don't-do-it, list-it person if I ever saw one. Let's go."

"But, Patti . . ." I followed Patti out of the cab and toward the station. "But, Patti, I've got stuff in there. A poem, and . . . just things. Anyway, she might *read* it. And Roger, too."

"Oh, sweetie, I am sorry." Patti dropped her suitcase and turned around, while people hurried past us. "And now you don't have another copy. We'll write a letter and ask her to mail it along. Come on, we'll look for another notebook in the station. Maybe one of those that look like a book but with empty pages inside."

I turned around to get one last look at Nicholas Fazenhiemer, only there were no cabs in sight. If I hadn't been in such a hurry to get us out of there, I might have remembered the journal. It was all my fault. But I was still glad we'd left. I followed Patti into the station.

"Maybe we should go back," said Patti, putting the lid back on her empty coffee cup.

"Go back where?"

"To the apartment. To Roger and Margey's. They don't know we've left, so they wouldn't have to know we'd come back. It would be as if we'd been there all along." She looked away from me and said, "You could even get your journal back," in a dangling kind of a way.

I felt as if I were jumping rope and someone had suddenly changed direction on me. "No. You can't do that. You can't go back. They didn't want us there, and besides—what would people think—the lady at the switchboard and that guy outside polishing the brass. Maybe Roger's home by now, and there we'd be, tromping in." The whole time I was saying it, I was caring about the journal, but knowing there was something else I cared about more.

"You worry too much what people think," said Patti, taking hold of the handle of the suitcase, her eyes darting toward the main concourse as though measuring the distance to the outside, to the taxi stand, to the apartment.

"Nicholas Fazenhiemer, we don't need you. Keep

driving. Keep away," I thought, picking up the other suitcase and reaching for the basket and the sleeping bag. I sat there poised, ready to jump if Patti jumped, to run if Patti ran. Ready to hurl myself between my mother and the whole of New York City.

"Now boarding at Gate 9—the 1:30 Metroliner for Newark: Trenton: 30th Street Station, Philadelphia: Wilmington: Baltimore: and Washington," a voice squawked from somewhere overhead. "Now boarding at Gate 9 . . ." There was a great surge of people swarming around us, and I edged Patti out into the crowd, so that we were caught up and carried along and bumped and bundled down the stairs on to the train.

"Well, all I can say is Margey may be your cousin, but she's a lousy hostess," said Patti as she sat on a high stool in Angel's kitchen.

I stood leaning in the doorway, feeling as though I had pushed the train all the way from New York to Baltimore. I heard Patti talking as if from far away, telling how it was her idea to leave New York, which was okay too; I watched Angel take extra pieces of chicken out of the freezer and hold them under running water, then drop them on the plate with the already thawed pieces. Even the earlier parts of the day seemed muzzy: the train ride; the taxi to Angel and Sid's and the wait on their front steps for Angel to get home from work, from picking Tommy up at day care. The water running in the sink, and cartoons from the TV in the living room had a wrapped-in-cotton sound.

"Anybody knows you can't just jump into a job in New

York or anywhere else, but I had the distinct feeling that we weren't welcome," Patti said.

"Well, it is hard, I suppose. Having guests, I mean, with Roger in school and Margey working and all. Their place is small, from what I hear." Angel concentrated on drying the chicken with a paper towel without once looking at Patti.

"Oh, it *is* small," said Patti, turning up her nose and looking around the kitchen as if that were under discussion too. "But it's not as though we needed to be entertained. You'd hardly have known we were there."

Angel reached over Patti to get the flour canister, started to say something, then seemed to bite her lip without actually biting it. She looked up and saw me watching her and said, "Why don't you go in and watch TV with Tommy. Get him to tell you about day care, only he calls it school."

I stood there for a minute, not sure whether Angel was really telling me to go, or whether she thought I liked cartoons, or even four-year-olds. Then I moved away from the door, trying to act casual—as if I were going because I wanted to go. But all the time feeling clumsy and in the way.

The living room was dark, with the kind of shadows that are caught in a room when the shades have been down all day. There were newspapers heaped on the couch and a half-eaten piece of jelly toast on the coffee table. Tommy's pajamas and his rabbit slippers made a little pile in front of the television where I was sure he had stepped out of them while watching his morning shows.

"Hey, Tommy," I said to the child lying on the floor. "How was school?"

Tommy looked over his shoulder at me and then turned

81

back to the set without saying anything. I sat down on the end of the couch and then got up again, not at all sure what I was supposed to be doing. I looked at the pictures on the top of the bookcase, leaning forward to peer at faces I didn't even know. I thought about calling Mary Jane to say that I was back and that maybe if she hadn't finished the aquarium play we could get together over the weekend. I remembered that Angel's telephone was in the kitchen. Then one thought just led to another: how we no longer had our apartment, and maybe I wouldn't even go back to the same school, or see Mary Jane again at all.

I moved on around the room, stepping over Tommy and heading back to the kitchen. Suddenly I wanted to move past the door, out into the center of the room, and stand on Tommy's little step stool and say, "Hey, everybody, look at me. I'm here. I'm somebody. H, my name is Henley, and I come from Henlopen, and I eat hen's eggs." I didn't, though.

There I was, hugging the edge of the mattress, hoping that Tommy wouldn't wet the bed and wishing that I could have slept in the living room with Patti. I felt myself slipping into sleep and shook my head, blinking my eyes to try to stay awake. I catalogued the rest of the day's events, saying them under my breath against the background of Tommy's snuffled breath. "Ate dinner and helped Angel with the dishes and watched Patti get ready to go out and read a story to Tommy, only he didn't say anything and Angel says be glad because once he starts talking he won't shut up. Took a bath and Angel let me use her bubble bath and went to bed because I didn't know what else to do and waited for Patti to come home to see what we are going to do."

I thought I heard the noise of a car door and propped my head up on my hand and listened, holding myself still and feeling my hand get numb. Everything was quiet. My head felt heavy and my eyelids drooped. I jerked forward and continued my list: "Took a bath and went to bed and waited for Patti to come home to see if she saw Eric . . . if she heard about an apartment . . . waited for Patti to come home . . ."

The next morning I woke up with Tommy sitting on top of me. He had finally decided to talk. "Hey, girl—you want to watch cartoons? It's Saturday and there's *Tom and Jerry* and *Bugs Bunny* and we can have jelly bread and cereal and you get to pour the milk—first you put it from the bottle to the fat-lady pitcher and then into the bowl, so come *on*." I rolled over on my back, toppling Tommy onto the other half of the bed and blinking at the light.

"What time is it?" I asked, scrabbling around in my head for the night before as if it were something I had misplaced.

"Time for *Tom and Jerry*, only it's halfway over by now. I turned it on already. Your mother's smoking cigarettes and mine's making coffee and she's making faces too. Like this." And he hooked his fingers under his eyes and pulled at the skin at the same time he jutted his bottom teeth out as far as they would go. "Because of the cigarettes, I guess. Daddy doesn't smoke anymore. And besides, it stinks.

Come on." He started for the door, then came back, rocking on his stomach across the bar at the foot of the bed and saying, "She said get dressed right now and bring your stuff and come on. I think you're going someplace."

When I got downstairs, the silence was pulled tight across the kitchen like the skin of a drum, and for a moment I wanted to keep going: following Tommy into the living room and stretching out on the floor beside him.

"Get your stuff. We're going. It's time to go," said Patti.

"Let the child have some breakfast," said Angel, pouring a glass of orange juice.

"She's not a child," snapped Patti.

"Of course she's a child, and probably a hungry one."

"We'll go to McDonald's. They don't lecture you at McDonald's. No rules tucked into the Egg McMuffin. No regulations in the pancakes and sausage."

"I didn't lecture. I just asked you to think things out," said Angel, sliding the glass across the counter to me.

I had it halfway to my lips when Patti said, "Think things out? 'Running off half-cocked' is what you said. 'Not fair to Henley' is what you said. 'Dragging her over hell's half-acre' is what you said."

I put the untouched glass of juice back on the counter.

"What I *said*—and I didn't think you'd mind, because we're friends—what I *said* was that sometimes it helps to think things out ahead of time. That it isn't always fair to Henley, yanking her from one place to the next. Kids need a place to live that isn't always moving out from under them like some kind of damn escalator, and a school that's more than a way station, and friends to grow up with."

I wanted to run forward and throw my arms around Angel and say, "That's right—that's how it is." At the same time I wanted to stand up next to Patti and say, "Leave her alone. That's the way Patti is and that's okay."

"Next you'll push for apple pie and early spring," said Patti, lighting another cigarette.

"There's nothing wrong with apple pie," said Angel.

"Dreary," said Patti. "Besides, Henley's tough—aren't you, Henny-penny?"

"Running her up to New York and back all in the same week—what kind of life is that for a kid?"

"She loved it there."

"Then why'd you leave?" said Angel.

"She wanted to leave. It was Henley's idea."

And there I was, jumping rope in my head and someone had changed direction again.

Angel went right on as if she hadn't heard. "Honestly, Patti—you have to give things a chance. Things don't happen all at once. Sometimes . . ."

But Patti was pushing herself away from the table and looking around the kitchen, at the eggs on the counter and Tommy's fat-lady pitcher and the orange peels in the sink. "And *this* is a happening?" she asked.

"Yes, yes, yes," said Angel. "This is a kind of happening." She piled honey buns on a plate and held them out to me and I took one and then was afraid to eat it, as if the very act of biting it would be taking Angel's side against Patti. She moved the plate to Patti. "Come on, have one. I didn't mean to upset you. Oh, I don't know, Patti. Maybe we're all partly to blame—the way we would be in and out of your place on weekends—always ready to get together, for a kind of party. Only, for the rest of us it was just a diversion—there was something else, too. Something to go back to. Maybe we haven't been much help to you. To you and Henley."

Patti jumped up, sending the chair clattering over backward. "Help? Help? We don't need your help. Yours or Sid's or Eric's or Margey's or anybody else's. We don't need anybody. Henley and I don't."

Before I knew what was what, Patti was through the hall, picking up her suitcase and the knapsack as she went, and out the door.

I stood for a moment and watched her run down the walk and throw her stuff into the back of the orange Volkswagen. It was as though I were watching a stranger, as if I had been passing a window and had seen someone come out of one of the other houses and get into a car.

Suddenly Patti and the stranger merged into one and I began to shake and I shoved the honey bun into my mouth and grabbed my things and nodded to Angel as I went.

I ran down the walk toward the car, afraid that at any minute Patti might put her foot on the accelerator and drive away.

I stopped still. For one awful moment I stood there and thought about the running and the pulling back and forth and the chasing after Patti. And, further back in my mind, I wondered what would happen if I didn't. If I let Patti drive away.

The bun dropped out of my mouth and I kicked it from where it had landed on the walk. Kicked it so hard it went spinning out and into a tree trunk and ricocheted off, breaking—as if in slow motion—into a splattering of honey-coated pieces and falling to the ground.

I ran after Patti and pulled open the door and got into the car just as she was pulling away.

eight

I've always had the feeling, from looking at those maps that hang in front of classrooms, that if you head north it's uphill; but if you go south you can coast all the way. We were going south and as Patti turned the car off the beltway and onto what the sign said was Maryland 3 it was as if we had picked up our feet and were careening along.

We rocketed off the ramp and onto the highway, veering from the right lane into the left and then back into the right again. We swung around a road-construction site, clipping an orange rubber cone and sending it spinning off into a field. We skimmed pockmarks in the road, bounced over bridges spanning culverts, and splattered gravel as we dipped onto the shoulder.

I dug my fingers into the underneath part of my legs as the car swerved on another ramp, and I was flung sideways toward Patti. I tried to sneak a look at the speedometer but was bumped back against the seat as the car hurtled onto Mountain Road and straightened out.

Inching my feet forward, I braced them against the floorboard and took a deep breath, turning to look at Patti. I let my breath ooze out a little at a time, letting it seep out around my teeth and between my lips, afraid that even a too-big push of air would send Patti, the car, and me bouncing across the grass strip in the middle of the road— into I didn't know what. I looked at her sharp-angled profile and the hair lashing against her face; her fingers, clenched white on the steering wheel. Then I faced forward, as Patti faced forward, and stared at the road spinning out in front of us.

From Mountain Road, Patti swung onto Ritchie Highway, which is definitely a trafficky kind of road, the car going along like shot from a cannon. We sped past McDonald's and Gino's and a White Coffee Pot Junior—a real fast-food heaven; past bowling alleys and Dairy Queens and houses crouched back away from the road. We stopped at traffic lights, screeching in at the very last second, and starting again just as the light was changing. We passed cars and motorcycles and a truck filled with chickens in crates. I tried to read the road signs and latch on to them in my head before they were whisked away—Annapolis, Cape St. Clair, Bay Bridge.

The car rattled and shook and I pushed back against the seat as we circled down onto Route 50 and headed for the Bay Bridge. I remembered how we came this way with Eric last summer, how Patti had had me close my eyes till we got to the top of the bridge, then open them, and how she had told me I was Henley on top of the world.

89

I wouldn't close my eyes now. It was as though, just by staring straight ahead at the road, I could keep everything okay. Patti dug in her bag and pulled out her wallet, balancing it on the steering wheel. As the car swerved, she righted it and tossed the wallet into my lap, still without saying anything. I put the money for the toll in her hand just as we slid to a stop at the toll booth. We waited for the red light to flash "thank you" and then Patti took a deep breath and started the car again. It was as though that breath were easing the car along—up, up, up onto the bridge, over the sand and the rocks of the jetty and the whitecaps on the bay. The really weird thing about it was that, no matter how fast we were going, another part of me was moving slowly and deliberately and seeing everything along the way. Like one of those games where somebody puts a whole bunch of things on a tray and you have to remember them and name them back again. But this didn't feel like a game. We went higher and higher, over sailboats and powerboats and freighters hugging the channel, onto the part of the bridge that was crisscrossed with shadow and sunlight made by the arches overhead, out over the nubbly surface that hummed against the tires and tickled the soles of my feet.

The car climbed to the very crest, and then Patti stopped, pulling up the handbrake and rolling the window down all the way. For a moment the car and the bridge itself seemed to sway beneath us.

"Well," said Patti, speaking for the first time since we had left the city. "We're out of that."

"Out of what?"

"Out of Angel's lecturing and Sid's dirty looks and Margey's saying 'Get a job, Patti,' and Roger and . . ."

Suddenly I wanted to take hold of Patti by the shoulders and shake her until the two of us and the little orange Volkswagen and even the bridge toppled down into the bay. I felt words drumming against the inside of my lips that wanted to say, "How come I can see it when you can't see it. That they're just trying to help, that you're just going round and round like a dog chasing its tail, and when somebody tells you to stop, you just turn and run the other way. How come I can see that when I'm the kid and you're the mother. And how come I don't know what else to do except to keep on going the way you keep on going. But the whole time I'm doing it, it's as if I know something I don't know I know."

On the top of the bridge, horns blew and cars darted around us and drivers glared and shook their fists and called back out of open windows. I thought that at any minute the bridge guards were going to come after us. I definitely didn't feel like Henley on top of the world.

"Where are we going now?" I asked, making my voice sound flat.

"Everywhere," said Patti, starting the car and turning on the radio. "Everywhere. Anywhere. Nowhere." We started down the far side of the bridge, faster and faster. As we went, Patti began to sing in time with the radio. The wind from the open window pushed against my face and made a roaring noise in my ears.

We stopped at Stuckey's, sitting at a picnic table under a tree to eat hamburgers and watch the traffic rush by, as if it were any old kind of a day and we were any old kind of people.

"Relax, Henny-penny," said Patti, reaching over and stabbing a pickle off my plate. "Relax and enjoy it."

"But, Patti—we have to be going someplace."

"We'll go where we go."

"But where's that? You have to know. I mean, people just don't . . ."

"People don't . . . People do. Tweedledum . . . Tweedle-dee."

"You must know *something*," I said. "Something about where we're going now." I looked at Patti with a long hard look and I saw the way she had torn her paper plate into ragged shreds.

"I told you. Somewhere. Anywhere. Everywhere. Nowhere. That's where we're going now," she said.

"That's not a place—a real place, where people live."

"Round and round and round she goes—where she stops, nobody knows," said Patti in a singsong voice.

We started off again, skimming through towns and over railroad crossings, at times ducking off the highway onto back roads, then catching up to the main road a few miles farther on. We went past an overhead sign that said "St. Michaels" and Patti slammed on the brakes and pulled to the side of the road, waiting for a lull in the traffic, and backed up to the cutoff.

"Maybe that's all we need—to get away from the city,"

she said, turning the steering wheel hard to the right and bearing down on the accelerator. "Maybe we'll find some place and just stop. That's what comes of traveling light. Instant housekeeping."

I wasn't listening anymore. My head throbbed with Patti's refrain: round and round and round she goes—where she stops, nobody knows. I closed my eyes and seemed to be surrounded by spinning things: a top, a windmill, a merry-go-round.

In St. Michaels we bought tickets for the Maritime Museum, but at the last minute Patti decided not to go in. "Tourists," she said, her lips curling at the edges. "On buses—probably with box lunches." She tore the tickets into tiny pieces and tossed them into the wind. As I watched them blow away, I thought about one of those tourist buses and in my imagination was just settling down with a set of grandparents—and their box lunch—when I felt Patti pull at me.

"Come on," she said, gesturing to the line outside the Crab Claw. "We'll go someplace else to eat—keep going. You can't make time waiting in line."

"Time for what?" I said, kicking at oyster shells in the road. "What's the point of hurrying when we're not going anyplace?"

But Patti was already out in front of me, running toward the car.

We spent the night in a motel, and the next morning Patti stayed in bed late—not sleeping exactly, but just staring up at the ceiling with her eyes half-closed. It wasn't until the maid opened the door with her passkey and practically pulled the chain out, saying that we had already stayed past checkout time and she was going to tell the manager, that we finally left.

We were heading east toward the ocean until at the last minute Patti veered south onto Route 113. I think what we were doing was making crisscrosses over the same territory. We could have been there a lot sooner than we were, except, of course, we weren't going anywhere.

"Ghost towns," said Patti, picking up her feet as we rattled over railroad tracks. "Make a wish, Henny-penny. When you pass a railroad crossing, pick up your feet and make a wish."

"I wish we'd stop," I said, with my feet firmly planted on the floor.

"Here? Stop here? Ye gods, there aren't even any people. The last three towns in a row, all we've seen are chickens. We'll stop when there's something to stop for. I told you that."

We stopped for gas, and at a diner for lunch, and at a stand by the side of the road where we looked at empty bottles and books with moldy covers and chairs without seats.

We followed a sign that said "Chincoteague," turning off the main road and bouncing along toward the east, past fields stubby with soybean plants, and houses with wrap-around front porches and shacks tumbled by the side of the road.

"Smell the salt air," said Patti, turning her face to the open window. "I always wanted to live by the sea—'I must go down to the sea again . . .' Aunt Mercy lives by the sea —in a town on the water."

"Aunt Mercy does?" I was suddenly alert. But Patti didn't seem to hear me, as the car went into a fit of shimmying and shaking and jolted up onto the bridge and down the other side, into the town.

"Motels cost money," I said, coming out of the bathroom and taking giant steps across the floor to the foot of the bed. "Even crummy ones that smell and have spots on the floor where people probably threw up. Restaurants cost money, too. And gas stations. We probably don't have any left and all our clothes are dirty and we ought to go to the laundromat, only we don't. We just keep going and getting nowhere."

"Lecture time," said Patti, twirling the dial of the television set and humming under her breath.

"But, Patti . . ."

"But, Patti, my foot. 'But, Patti, the motel is crummy.' "

"It stinks."

"And we're spending too much money, but if we stayed someplace better, we'd be spending more money, so what do you think of that, my fine-feathered Henny-penny?"

"I think I'm tired," I said, all of a sudden feeling like a balloon with the air whooshed out. I flopped back on the bed and tried not to notice the stale, musty smell.

"Tired—you're tired? My God, all you have to do is sit in the car and everything is done for you. Tired? Tired? What do you mean, tired? What about me? What about what I'm tired of?"

I heard Patti's voice getting higher and higher. I knew that I should do something to break the pattern of her words, but it was as though I was trapped—caught in an undertow. I'm tired . . . you're tired? . . . tired of going anywhere . . . what do you have to be tired for . . . and getting nowhere . . . tired . . . tired . . . tired . . .

The next morning I woke up carefully, as if there were something I ought to know and couldn't quite remember. I saw that Patti's side of the bed was empty and heard water running in the bathroom and closed my eyes again, trying to sort waking from sleeping.

I moved tentatively through the night before, through the heavy darkness of the motel room broken only by the gap in the curtains and the glow of Patti's cigarette. I seemed to see my mother huddled at the table and felt the grittiness of the spotted carpet on my knees as I knelt beside her and held on to her while Patti said over and over, "I'm so scared, Henny-penny. I'm so scared." I probed at my remembering, not quite sure whether or not I had stayed with Patti in my arms until daylight edged the curtains and the ashtray was spilling over with cigarette butts.

"Come on, get up," said Patti, coming out of the bathroom already dressed. "I've thought it all out—how we'll get an early start—head out of here. Find somewhere with a little life, a little class. We'll go back the way we came."

I pulled on my clothes, gathered my belongings, and followed Patti outside. Just as the door slammed shut, I saw out of the corner of my eye the ashtray, overflowing with cigarette butts and pushed into the middle of the table.

The morning sun was hot; the air was still; the car stuffy with a peanut-butter smell from the pack of crackers propped on the dashboard.

"We'll get out of here first, before we eat. Get away from this town," said Patti as the car shuddered and lurched its way out onto the road. We crossed the bridge, going past the workboats in dock and the rowboats up-turned along the marsh. The car quivered as Patti pushed down on the gas, and for a long time we seemed to race along. We fairly flew over a bump in the road and my stomach flip-flopped inside me. Then, gradually, the blur of fields and telephone poles sharpened into focus.

"Damn," said Patti, pumping hard on the accelerator and shaking the steering wheel. "Damn. Damn. Damn. Damn."

The orange Volkswagen drifted to a stop beside a field.

nine

"We can't just walk away and leave it," I said, looking up ahead at the car, which wavered in the sunlight and seemed to recede the closer we got to it, as if someone had it by a string and was yanking it just out of reach.

"You heard what that man at the gas station said. It sounds like the transmission, and transmissions cost hundreds of dollars and we don't *have* hundreds of dollars. We don't even have *one* hundred dollars anymore."

"But we could have it towed. He said he'd tow it in and look at it. He really can't tell just by your telling him about it."

"Oh, he can tell, all right," said Patti, opening her eyes wide and staring just beyond me. "They're all seers and sorcerers and psychics. That's how they get jobs in gas stations in the first place. They see into motors and under hoods and know about rattles and gasps and what that awful noise means. We just walked on down there and told him and even from half a mile down the road he knew. This way we don't have to pay to tow it. Besides—once they got it there, they'd expect us to *do* something about it. You heard what he said anyway—about how the Trailways bus comes through here. Stopping at the store at the next crossroads up. We haven't been anywhere by bus in a long time. We'll just get our suitcases and go along and wait for the bus."

I started to say a lot of things, such as how sensible people didn't just abandon cars by the side of the road. And what about our belongings stuffed into leaf bags and crammed in the back seat. And even if we left the car, why wouldn't somebody be able to check the license number and trace it to us that way—except then I remembered we really weren't anyplace that we could be traced to. That being next to an empty field between here and there was the same as being nowhere.

Patti opened the trunk and threw the two suitcases out on the side of the road. She rummaged in the front seat, sifting through road maps and Tastykake wrappers, found her sunglasses and an extra pack of cigarettes, and shoved them down into her knapsack. I flipped the seat forward and stood for a minute staring at the clutter in the back of the car. I ran my fingers over the piece of driftwood we had found last summer, and lightly touched the frazzled cuff of my baggy maroon sweat shirt sticking out of the top of a bag. I pulled out my basket and a canvas bag of books and set them on the ground and reached for the large framed picture of the white rabbit that had hung in my room wherever we had lived.

"Oh no, you don't," said Patti, nudging the canvas bag with her foot. "Books are heavy, and this time we're really traveling light. You can forget about that damn white rabbit."

"No," I said. "No." I stamped my feet and watched the dust from the side of the road cloud up and then settle again, turning my dark-blue tennis shoes a chalky white. "I—will—not—leave—my—books." I kicked the bag with one foot, moving it over in back of me. "I'll carry them myself, and it doesn't matter how heavy they are, I won't ever put them down. Even if my arms fall out. There's *The Secret Garden* and *The Wind in the Willows* and *Wrinkle in Time* and *Caddie Woodlawn* and all the good stuff."

We stood facing each other and I saw the frantic look in Patti's eyes. But I couldn't give in. I stood with my body partway shielding the bag, and right away I knew that, no matter how important they were, it was more than a matter of books. After a minute I turned toward the car and gave the white rabbit a shove, sending it toppling against the sleeping bag. I slammed the car door, hefting the canvas bag, my basket, and the knapsack, and started up the road, calling back over my shoulder, "See—I told you they weren't heavy. Told you I could carry them."

I heard a shuffling in back of me and turned to see Patti running up the road carrying the suitcases. When she came alongside of me, she broke into a loose-jointed kind of dance, just like a rag doll, which got floppier and wilder. As she passed she turned to face me and continued to dance backward up the road.

> *"Oh, we ain't got a barrel of money,*
> *Maybe we're ragged and funny,"*

she sang.

> *"But we'll travel the road,*
> *Sharing our load.*
> *Side by side."*

She waited for me to catch up and traded the basket for one of the suitcases, looping elbows and jogging me along, the way they do in those old movies you see on TV.

> *"Through all kinds of weather—*
> *What if the sky should fall . . ."*

We rounded the curve in the road and came in sight of a white ramshackle store with a gas pump out in front and a faded Trailways sign hanging overhead. Patti hustled me along faster and faster, whistling the rest of the verse. We swerved off the road onto the gravel gouged deep with tire tracks. Patti let go of me, throwing her arms up in the air and saying, "That's it. The sky is falling, Henny-penny. The sky is falling and we have to hurry and tell the king."

I watched Patti dart into the store, the screen door slapping shut, then flopping partway open again. I put down the suitcase and the bag and flexed my fingers, rubbed them against the side of my shorts, and I followed Patti into the store.

Inside, it was dark and cool and smelled of licorice. "Who's the king?" I asked, going to stand beside Patti at the glass-fronted case.

"When's the next bus north—to anywhere?" Patti asked the woman sitting behind the counter.

"Who's the king, Patti?" I asked.

Patti drummed her fingers on the glass-cover top over the sour balls and Mary Janes and red licorice strings in that way she had when she'd heard exactly what someone said —only wanted to pretend she hadn't.

The woman peered out at us, as if she thought people ought to know which way they wanted to go, then looked up at the Coca-Cola clock, then out toward the door as if she expected to find a Trailways bus lurking there.

"The bus north's gone already," she said. "Nine-seventeen this morning, same as every morning."

The three of us stood there in silence for a moment, listening to a dog barking outside, as if the way that dog was barking was really important. Then the woman went on, "Only other bus be by at ten after one, but it's heading on down the shore. You interested in that? Stops at Temperanceville . . . Accomac . . . Onley . . . Exmore . . . Eastville, and . . ."

"Yes," said Patti, pushing money across the top of the candy counter. "Yes . . . yes . . . yes, that's fine. We'll have two for as far as it goes. Two to the end of the line." Then she turned toward me but didn't look *at* me. Instead, she looked up at the ceiling—at the rafters and the fan going round and round and the pieces of sticky paper hanging down all glopped up with bodies of flies. Dead ones. So that, forever after, when I thought of important things happening, I thought of flypaper. And Patti said, still looking at the ceiling, "The king is Aunt Mercy. The sky is falling, Henny-penny, and it looks like we're going to tell the king."

We sat on cinder blocks out in front of the store and ate butterscotch crimpets and drank orangeade and waited for the bus to come. I gathered up the trash and tossed it into the green metal can, then stalked a scruffy gray kitten along the side of the store, watching as it disappeared under a rusted chaise. When it didn't come back, I continued on around the building, back to where I had started, and went to stand in front of Patti.

"I don't remember it all that well," I said, staring down at her. "The story about Chicken-licken and Henny-penny and Ducky-lucky and all those guys. What I don't remember is—when the sky is falling, does the king tell them what to do?"

"I hope so," said Patti in a faraway voice, and right away I hoped so, too. More than anything in the whole wide world. "But I think it depends on how you tell the story— whether the fox eats everybody up, in a cave, and comes out picking his teeth—or whether the king explains it all, tells them it's not the sky but only some lousy acorn." Patti moved her shoulders into a shrug, but instead of letting them go, she kept them hunched as she said, "You're the story-teller, Henny-penny. Maybe it's up to you to find the ending."

Suddenly I was scared. This story was different from any of the others I had ever told myself before; different from the mummies and the Nicholas Fazenhiemer story or the aquarium play I had never had a chance to write— but could have. Different from all the stories I knew I was going to write someday. It was as though I were moving on to something I wasn't ready to move on to yet. I squirmed my feet into the hot dusty ground so I could make myself feel real again, and looked right at Patti and said, "Does Aunt Mercy want us to come? Will she be glad? Shouldn't we call her up and see if it's okay in case she's going somewhere. And if it's not too far, maybe she'll bring us back to get the stuff—the white-rabbit picture and the Christmas decorations."

But Patti was already standing up, shielding her eyes from the sun and pointing up the road as the red-and-silver bus lumbered toward us, making the ground shake beneath our feet.

The bus hummed monotonously along, pulling into each little town, stopping briefly, and then heading on to the next one. There was a sameness about the towns that made me wonder if the driver was just looping in some great circle: past the same granite gray bank and grocery store; the same lunchroom and Exxon station and Dollar General.

I closed my eyes and rested my head against the back of the seat, then jerked suddenly forward as if it mattered that I keep track of where we were going—if, in fact, we were going anyplace at all. I let my head drop back on the seat again. "H, my name is Henley . . ." I said over and over to myself as I stared out the window at the fields stretching flat and endless on both sides of the road.

Standing on the sidewalk by the side of the bus, I brushed myself off. I felt jolted, as if I had been sitting on a giant's lap and the giant had suddenly stood up, sending me sideslipping onto the ground. All along that flat white road the bus-giant had held Patti and me, rocking and lulling us; carrying us to Aunt Mercy's. Now we stood in front of the Pop Shop while the driver ground the bus into gear and made a U-turn in the middle of the street and headed back the way he had come. I felt abandoned. I wanted to run after the bus, pound on the side, catch hold of the door, pry it open with my fingers, pull my way up the two steep steps, clamor down the aisle. I wanted to curl up in my seat by the window with my eyes closed and burrow into the rhythm of the wheels. When I turned to look at Patti, it was as though I was looking into a mirror: all my feelings were reflected in her face. She reached out her hand, stepping off the curb into the street. Then the bus was gone and I was tugging at her arm, saying, "Which way now? Which way to Aunt Mercy's?"

Patti turned back and looked at me, blinking for a moment as if to clear her eyes of other sights. Then, without saying anything, she gathered her things and led the way up Main Street, away from the Pop Shop. She turned at the corner and went on past the post office, stopping in front of the Bayview Hotel, pausing as if trying to remember the way. She went up Plum Street, past houses with silent faces and empty porches, turned at the Baptist church, went over to Mulberry Street, stopping at the wide steps of the Presbyterian church. I followed along behind her.

"Churches," she said. "That's what I remember. Churches everywhere. A church on every corner. Baptists and Presbyterians. The Catholics are over there somewhere.

And the Episcopalians are up ahead. There must be more. Even the library's a church—or used to be." Patti pulled a brush out of her knapsack, bending at the waist, brushing and setting up a great swirl of hair. She straightened up and shoved her shirt down into her skirt. I saw that her hands were shaking and there were two spots of color on her cheeks.

Patti started to hand me the brush, but at the last minute she pulled it back, reaching instead to smooth the wisps of hair around my face, the way she had done when I was a little girl. For a minute I wanted to be that little girl again. And didn't want to be. Did and didn't both at the same time. Then I yanked the brush out of Patti's hand and brushed my own hair as hard as I could until my scalp was burning. Patti just stood there looking at me, and after a while she said, "Remember, Henny-penny. What I've told you about being special and making something out of all this mess. Oh, and all the things I guess I've always wanted you to know. Hey, and one thing you'd better never forget—you're not just anybody's kid. Remember that. Now come on. Aunt Mercy, here we come, ready or not."

When we got to the block after the library, I felt that I was leading the way, that it was Patti who was hanging back, dragging her feet. At the corner I almost had to shove Patti across the street.

Once we were on the other side she stopped, dropping her suitcase and turning to face back the way we had come. "Maybe we shouldn't go. Maybe we should just go back. Wait and catch another bus." I saw Patti's face, which had been splotched with color, and was now a flat, grayish white.

I stood looking at the houses that lined both sides of the street. "It's that one, isn't it? The white house on that side, with the green steps and the bushes across the front. I know it from the stories you used to tell." I started up the street, looking straight ahead, and somehow I sensed, rather than saw, that Patti was walking along beside me.

"Look." I started to run. "There's the porch, and the swing, and there's somebody there. Somebody in the swing."

As I turned into the walk, I felt Patti pressing close against me. The suitcases, the knapsack, the basket, and the canvas bag of books caught around our feet and stopped us at the bottom of the steps.

The woman sat hunched in the swing looking down at us. She held her hands under her chin, her right hand stroking her left as though it were a small and helpless animal; her feet were crossed at the ankles and hung above the floor. She rocked back and forth in a kind of counterpoint to the rhythm of the swing.

"Is that Aunt Mercy?" I asked out loud.

"Of course not," said Patti, kicking at the clutter of things around our feet. "That's Booshie. She lives here, too —is still here—"

At the sound of her name, the woman got off the swing and sidled across the porch, bobbing her head up and down and stroking her hand faster and faster.

Patti dug her fingers into my arm and put her foot on the bottom step and called, "Hi, Booshie. It's me—Patti— and I've come home."

Up above I saw the woman who was called Booshie nodding and rocking and whimpering as she stood with her back against the door.

ten

For a minute I didn't think Booshie was going to let us go inside. She guarded the door of Aunt Mercy's house the way the three-headed dog Cerberus had guarded the gates of Hades in my last year's mythology book. And I wondered, if Booshie let us in at all, if she would, like Cerberus, devour us, so that we would never come out again.

I poked Patti in the ribs, hissing and rolling my eyes at her as if to say, "Come on; let's get out of here. You were right when you said we shouldn't have come. We should just go back . . . catch another bus." But by that time Patti had gathered our belongings and was moving forward, pressing on so that there was nothing for Booshie to do but open the door and creep inside just ahead of her. The screen door swung and cracked me on the elbow as I grabbed for my basket and followed Patti into the hall.

Inside, the darkness gradually sorted itself into shapes: a fireplace and a hat rack and a bust of an Indian girl resting on a wooden pedestal. I blinked and the hall began to brighten into splotchy red and blue and yellow patches as the sunlight filtered through the stained-glass windows lining the stairs.

Booshie stood against the hat rack, her back to the mirror, so that I could see all of her at once. My stomach lurched and I shuddered as I watched Booshie rock back and forth, back and forth. "Even old Cerberus would be an improvement over that," I thought as I tried to separate the doughy blob of a woman into an assortment of parts. Her head was bent over her hands and her gray-blond hair hung forward, parting at the back of her neck over skin that was raw and crusted red. Her checked cotton dress puckered at the shoulder seams, and in the front it spanned her spongy bosom and then hung straight and shapeless to the knees. She wore white ankle socks and black bedroom slippers that seemed to sigh as she rocked heel to toe.

She was about the toad-ugliest thing I had ever seen.

I tried to imagine brushing against her, touching her, reaching out with one finger and having that finger disappear into folds of pulpy flesh. My stomach did flip-flops again and I cringed and moved closer to Patti.

"Crazy," said Patti, twirling her finger at her head. "Loony. Nutty like a fruit cake. I can't believe she's still here—why Aunt Mercy keeps her here. Maybe that's why they called her Aunt Mercy in the first place."

"You said it's because her name is Mercedes."

"Her name *is* Mercedes, but try to tell it to the yokels around here. To them, Aunt Mercy is the same as saying

Aunt Doctor: Aunt Do-Good: Aunt Take Care. And wait until they take the sidewalks up. After supper they roll them right on up . . ."

It was as though Patti was taking the Aunt Mercy stories and pulling the stuffings out of them.

"But, Patti—you said . . ."

"I said—you said—we said. I scream—you scream—we all scream for ice cream. Loonies in the parlor and lions in cages on the walls. Anyway, we're here. We're here and the sky is falling, Henny-penny, and Aunt Mercy is going to kiss it and make it go away. Come on, I may as well show you around. This is the hall, and step right this way. In here we have—you're not going to believe this—in here we have the parlor. Used exclusively when company comes to call. The minister and maybe a burgomaster or two, except nobody has those anymore. Least of all, not on the Eastern Shore. The butcher, the baker, the candlestick maker."

I followed Patti into the parlor, with its windows across the front and up one side, a tall, narrow, gold-framed mirror reaching floor to ceiling, and the black upright piano standing stiff against the wall. I saw the three of us—Patti, Booshie, and me—captured in the surface of the mirror, and moved sideways, trying to pull away. But somehow I remained caught in the reflection as if the glass had angled out to catch the corners of the room. I saw the reverse image of the spinning wheel and the marble table with the gold ball feet, and the plush-covered chairs. I saw the turnabout of Booshie as she shuffled just in front of Patti: between Patti and the objects in the room.

Then I turned my back deliberately on the mirror, facing out into the room. I saw Booshie scuttle between Patti and the table in front of the windows, interrupting Patti as she reached for a blue glass slipper.

"It's still in the same spot it's always been in. Everything. The lamp, the slipper, the cracker jar. Nothing's changed," said Patti as she moved along to the piano, with Booshie moving right along with her as if playing some giant game of Keep Away.

"Oh, for crying out loud, what do you think I'm trying to do—steal the family heirlooms? Come on, let's see the library." Patti moved through the sliding doors that were swallowed back into the walls, into the next room, with Booshie dancing shuffle-footed ahead of her.

I stood at the door of the room, catching my breath at the walls of books and the warm musty smell of leather. Reaching out, I touched the backs of the books on the nearest shelf. Suddenly I was jostled off-balance: pushed backward, as Booshie forced her way between me and the shelf of books, saying, "No—no—no—no," over and over again in little breaths that smelled of graham crackers.

Across the room, Patti flopped on the couch, her shoulders jolting against the back, her feet flying out in front. There was a bristling, crunching sound beneath her.

"Horsehair. Good God, I'd forgotten horsehair. It's called a davenport, mind you. Nothing you'd want to curl up on for a nap, or anything else, for that matter. Keeps you on the straight and narrow, horsehair does."

Booshie darted back across the room, pulling at Patti, sidestepping left and right and then left again, her arms waving frantically until she managed to get them under control and hold them close to her, one hand stroking the other one.

We went into the dining room, which had an empty, discarded air about it. There was a yellow sweater dangling from a chair and a stack of papers on the sideboard next to a samovar, as if someone had dropped them on the way to some more important part of the house.

"We would have dinner in here—when I used to come. All of us together—around the table. Sherbet and lady-fingers and iced tea made with lemons and oranges and fresh-picked mint . . ." Patti's voice drifted off, and she stood with her fingers resting gently on the tabletop. For a minute her voice had lost its hardness and I heard an echo of the stories she used to tell.

But the moment was snatched away as Booshie moved in on Patti, swaying close to her and reciting, "Yellow dress yellow dress yellow dress," as if it were an incantation. "Yellow dress yellow dress . . ."

"There," said Patti, swinging sharply around and pointing to a picture on the wall—a picture of a lion in a heavy brown frame, with silver-painted bars on the outside of the glass and a lock fastened at the corner. "See—what did I tell you. Lions in cages on the walls, and loonies in the dining room."

"Lions and tigers and bears, oh my . . ." I said, looking up at the picture.

"Yellow dress yellow dress," repeated Booshie.

The kitchen was large and square and filled with sunlight. There were doors leading to the pantry and the back porch, the cellar and the back stairs, and to a room that angled out in back of the kitchen itself.

"There—she sleeps back there. Thank heavens, not upstairs," said Patti, rolling her eyes at Booshie and reaching out to start the bare light bulb hanging from a cord swaying back and forth across the table. Booshie followed Patti as she worked her way around the table. For a minute it seemed to me that the two of them were caught in a maze and would have to continue going around and around forever. Patti broke away, moving in a wider circle around the room, past the sink and the drainboard on spindly legs, the stove, a red-painted dresser, and a funny, old-fashioned radio that came to a point at the top and had a shiny brown fabric down the front. Booshie moved beside her like a shadow, her face ever watchful.

We went out of the kitchen in a kind of procession: Patti followed by Booshie, with me coming along behind. Through the door with the screen bellying out and covered over with a faded curtain, back through the dining room, past a tall, glass-paned door, and up one step into a kind of office.

In this room I suddenly felt the realness of Aunt Mercy. Felt it strongly and for the first time. As if she truly existed. I began to shape a person out of the worn rocking chair, the well-read books stacked and jumbled on tables and windowsills and spilling down onto the floor, the sturdy, bulky yellow-oak desk, and the daybed under the window. I learned more about her from the folded crossword puzzle on top of the little television set, the dictionary open on a stand, the empty coffee mug and the cookie tin, conch shells and a carved wooden sandpiper. All of Aunt Mercy seemed to come together and be focused on the wall of pictures behind the desk. I stopped and stood and stared at them.

There were a pair of shadowbox frames, deep and stiff, with a man and a woman peering out of them: formidable-looking—and somehow kind. There were gold and silver and wooden frames; large ones and small ones; doubles and triples; and a cascade of miniatures suspended from a wide black ribbon. I saw faces in faded brown, black-and-white, and color; girls on swings and seesaws and front porches; baby pictures, graduation pictures; and wedding pictures. Young men in knickers and white flannels and army uniforms. Children in party clothes, and the same children repeated inches, and years, along, in caps and gowns or holding children of their own.

I moved forward to see them better. It was as if the faces, the pictures, the frames, and the wall itself were drawing me toward them.

Then Booshie was in front of me. Swaying, shuffling, and fluttering in a fit of agitation. Pushing back at me and beckoning for Patti to come forward. She patted one hand with the other, then lurched toward the wall and pointed to a picture of a girl sitting on a porch rail, then back to Patti, then to the picture again. Her voice came as a whisper, at first hissing out of some secret place inside her, then spilling out into the room. "Barbara," she said. "Barbara. Barbara. Barbara."

She lunged toward Patti, her fingers pressing against Patti's chest, then jerking back. "Barbara. Barbara. Yellow dress yellow dress yellow dress . . ."

"Stop it," I yelled, breaking between them and watching my mother's face, which seemed to be disintegrating.

Behind me, I was conscious of the rhythm of Booshie as she rocked back and forth, whispering, "Yellow dress yellow dress . . ."

"Are there pictures of you on the wall?" I asked, still facing Patti. "Which one are you?"

"I'm not there," she said. "You know how I hate to have my picture taken. There was one once—over there— but I got mad at Aunt Mercy and tore it up."

The air stirred in back of me as Booshie rocked harder and harder.

"What do I want my picture up there for, anyhow?"

"Yellow dress yellow dress yellow dress . . ."

From the front of the house came the slap of a screen door, followed by the sound of footsteps. We were all suddenly quiet.

Then Patti broke away, running forward to the open glass-paned door and stopping in front of the small white-haired woman standing there. "Aunt Mercy—it's me— Patti. Another long-lost niece come home. I've brought my daughter, and her name is Henley." Her voice sounded young and breathless, as if she were giving someone the answers to a riddle.

"H, my name is Henley," I thought as I looked at Patti and at Aunt Mercy, who somehow didn't look large enough, or imposing enough—or Aunt Mercyish enough—to be Aunt Mercy.

Over against the wall, still looking at the picture of the girl on the porch, Booshie began to sway again, and to wail, "Yellow dress yellow dress . . ."

Aunt Mercy moved into the room, dropping her black doctor bag on the desk chair and going directly to Booshie, as if Patti and I weren't even there, taking her by the shoulders and stopping her rocking as she said, "All right. It's all right now." She propelled Booshie forward, away from the wall of pictures, toward the door and down into the dining room.

"Cookies. Booshie, we need cookies. We have guests and they are hungry. Booshie, you put the cookies on a plate. In the kitchen." She moved Booshie forward gently, until she took over on her own and continued toward the kitchen.

Then Aunt Mercy turned and looked from me to Patti. Her eyes, which were that startlingly clear kind of blue that go on forever, seemed to see us all around, the way I had seen Booshie in the mirror.

"Patti," she said, holding out her hands. "And Henley." Then, "Patti. Patti. Patti."

I saw my mother standing alone—like the cheese in a game of Farmer in the Dell. It was almost as though I could hear the clapping of hands and the scraping of feet as everybody backed away: the farmer, his wife, the dog, the cat, even the rat. And the cheese stands alone . . . the cheese stands alone.

Then it seemed that before my eyes the cheese—Patti, my mother—began to come apart, to crumble. She moved forward, toward Aunt Mercy, who was moving toward her. Aunt Mercy folded Patti in her arms, held her, rocked her, and turned and walked her out of the room, through the dining room toward the hall. All the while she was saying,

"There, there, there. You sleep until you can't sleep anymore. As for you, Miss Henley," she called back over her shoulder, "you go into the kitchen and help Booshie put the cookies on a plate. I'll be down in just a minute."

eleven

I didn't like Aunt Mercy.

Okay. So what. You can't like everybody, I told myself.

But this is Aunt Mercy, my self told me back. Of the Aunt Mercy stories.

I mean, it was like finding that the tooth fairy wore combat boots.

Here we had come to tell her the sky was falling, expecting Aunt Mercy to take the world and put it back together again, and all she had done was to hustle Patti off to bed and set me to serving cookies with some rocking-back-and-forth kind of crazy in the kitchen.

After Aunt Mercy took Patti upstairs, Booshie and I stood side by side at the kitchen table for a few minutes, listening to them moving overhead. Then Booshie took the cookies, one by one, out of the paper sack and lined them up on the plate. When the plate was full and the bag was empty, she reversed the process, returning the cookies to the sack: to the plate: to the sack again, until there was a fine dusting of crumbs along the tabletop and the edges of the cookies were blunted. When Aunt Mercy came down from settling Patti in bed, she waited, poised, until the plate was filled again, and then had Booshie pass it to me, to her, and she put it on the dresser. Right after that, she started getting supper ready. I stood first on one foot and then the other, while Aunt Mercy fried chicken and sliced tomatoes, and Booshie moved around the table, placing knives and forks, whispering, "Eighteen hundred and thirteen . . . eighteen hundred and . . ." Even when Aunt Mercy sent me into the pantry for milk, I was sure it was just busywork: they could have gotten along just as well without me.

By this time I was really mad, because Aunt Mercy didn't seem to know I was there. I sat at the round kitchen table with the bare light bulb swinging overhead and the cool slick feel of oilcloth on my fingers where it dipped down into my lap, and thought how I didn't like her at all. When it was time to say grace, Aunt Mercy and Booshie held hands, each stretching her other hand out to me. And what did I do? I sat on my hands, pushing down as hard as I could, leaving the two of them with their spare hands dangling. On the one side, Booshie inched her chair away from me, rocked, and counted, while Aunt Mercy said, "Oh, Heavenly Father, we thank you for this food . . ."

I stubbed my foot against the table leg and looked across at Booshie, who was chewing and counting all at the same time, so that little flecks of bread and spit formed in the corners of her mouth. Even when the food had disappeared down the back of her throat, Booshie kept right on counting and rocking, until she added another mouthful, then started to chew again. "Nineteen hundred and seventy-one . . . nineteen hundred and seventy-two . . . nineteen hundred and . . ."

There were all those stories Patti had told me when I was little—the Aunt Mercy stories—and I had always thought of them as my own private fairy tales. Now here I was on top of the golden mountain, or on the other side of the moat, and the fairy godmother didn't seem to care. She didn't even look the way I thought she would. Aunt Mercy was supposed to be seven and a half feet tall and with one hand be able to hold up the sky that was falling all around me, while with the other she was finding a cure for the common cold. A sort of combination Madame Curie and the Bionic Woman. Forget it. What I had instead was a tiny white-haired woman with a beaky sort of nose, her glasses dangling from a chain around her neck so that they clanked against her plate every time she leaned forward—with a blob of mayonnaise on the left lens. Another thing: nobody told me she had her own ogre, her own gargoyle, her own ugly old troll.

"Nineteen hundred and seventy-three . . . nineteen hundred and seventy-four . . ." said Booshie from the other side of the table.

Aunt Mercy passed the chicken to me and said, "Booshie is still making up her mind about you, Henley, but don't worry. I think it will be all right. She's a very loyal person, and once she decides she's on your side, she'll stick to you no matter what. Booshie never forgets."

"Like an elephant," I thought, poking at the drumstick on my plate and watching Booshie out of half-raised eyes.

"Ugly old troll-elephant-blobby thing—as if I wanted her to like me. As if I care." I watched Aunt Mercy lean forward and tug at Booshie's hand. "Look at me, Booshie. Look at me, and no more counting now."

"Twenty hundred and forty-one . . . twenty hundred and forty-two . . ."

"This is Henley, Booshie. Her name is Henley," Aunt Mercy said.

"H, my name is Henley," I thought.

"This is Patti's girl, and Patti brought her home to us."

She made me sound like a loaf of bread, or a bag of laundry.

"Yellow dress," said Booshie, looking at me and then up at the ceiling.

"She doesn't like my mother. She doesn't like Patti," I said. "So why do I want her to like me? Why is she all the time saying 'yellow dress'?"

"Twenty hundred and fifty-nine . . . twenty hundred and sixty . . ." Booshie rocked so furiously that the chair squeaked beneath her.

"She has her reasons," Aunt Mercy said. "But the thing about Booshie is that she is willing to accept every person as though she's never known anyone else before. A totally new experience, with none of the little tags of already-formed ideas that the rest of us carry from one person to the next. Once she makes up her mind, that is." She licked the mayonnaise off her glasses, rubbed at them with a paper towel, blew on them, and rubbed some more.

"How do you know she knows anything at all? What about the counting?"

Aunt Mercy looked quickly at Booshie, then back to

me. "The counting is a kind of security—something that goes on and on. Numbers never end. Sometimes she stops and starts again—sometimes she gets way up in the hundreds of thousands. But she never misses a number."

"Patti said she was crazy."

Aunt Mercy cracked her fingers down against the table's edge so hard that I felt the sting on my own hand clenched in a ball in my lap. "Never let me hear that word again. Never. We'll talk more about Booshie at a better time. I'll tell you what I know." She started to gather the dishes, and I could almost see the sparks flying, there among the plates, cups, saucers, and bowls. "Please, Booshie, clear the table, while I talk to Henley about her mother."

My face still burned as I stared down at the shreds of paper napkin in my lap. I made up my mind that I wouldn't ask her questions ever again. I didn't want to hear anything from her.

"About Patti," said Aunt Mercy, pouring more iced tea into her glass. "We'll let her rest—sleep on until morning. I want to run a few tests, make sure she's not anemic, because she seems generally rundown."

"She's not," I said, pushing my chair away from the table. "She's fine. Not sick or anything. It's just—just that we've been on the road a lot lately. We've had to go places and . . . and . . ." I wanted to cry. Suddenly it seemed that Aunt Mercy-the-Doctor was saying I hadn't taken care of Patti, that I had let her get rundown, maybe even anemic. I thought of all the times I told Patti to stop smoking, to start eating, and to go to bed. Then I had to stop thinking of all those things and concentrate on the lump that was growing inside my throat. I had to keep saying over and over inside myself, "I will not cry . . . I will not cry . . ." And for a minute I felt like Booshie, just rocking and counting. "I will not cry."

". . . get her straightened out as soon as we can," Aunt Mercy went on.

I was afraid to move, afraid of the tears that might suddenly spill over, afraid that if they did, they might never stop.

Booshie bumped against my shoulder. Thump. I blinked my eyes and focused them on the pattern of her dress just as she swung the plate of cookies in front of my face. She stood there swaying and watched as I looked at the cookies, as I slowly reached for one.

I held the cookie in my hand and wondered how I could get it past the thing growing in my throat.

"Cookie," said Booshie, leaning close to me and breathing her graham-cracker breath. "Cookie. Cookie."

I put the cookie in my mouth. Slowly I felt my throat relax, felt myself begin to chew. To swallow.

"Cookie," said Booshie. "Cookie. Cookie."

Booshie got ready to do the dishes as though she were preparing for surgery. Shrugging her way into a yellow cobbler's apron, she took out the broom, leaning it against the table. She filled the dishpan with soap and water, and held on to the spigots, swaying back and forth while the bubbles climbed in peaks. As she started to lift the glasses into the sink, she stopped, still counting under her breath, grabbed a towel off the rack, and shoved it at me.

"Good—she's going to let you help," said Aunt Mercy, picking up a book. "I was worried about that. You see, Booshie's very protective about the jobs that are hers. Particularly sweeping. She loves to sweep. I'm going to call the hospital and check on several patients, then I'll be out on the porch."

"Big deal," I thought as I shook out the towel, and grabbed the first plate from the rack. "Big deal—she's going to let me dry. Big deal—big deal. Just as long as I don't touch her precious broom."

I looked at Booshie's back, the yellow apron hanging loose over her already shapeless dress, shoulders hunched forward, the hands submerged in soapy water, moving rhythmically. I looked at the broom propped against the table. Instead of reaching for another plate, I inched closer to the broom and stretched out my hand. Then all of a sudden there was a great churning and splashing of water in the sink as Booshie jerked backward and forward. "Twenty-one hundred and seventy-five . . . twenty-one hundred and . . ."

I pulled my hand back as though it had been burned.

We sat on the north corner of the porch after supper: Booshie in the swing, Aunt Mercy in the tall green rocking chair, and me on the top step, my arms locked around my knees. We sat without talking, listening to the creaking of the swing and somewhere, from the back of one of the houses, the sound of voices—of someone calling, "All-y, all-y in free." For a minute I wanted to run across the street, around the side of the house, through hedges and over flower gardens to touch base.

I didn't move.

"Ho, there. Not out delivering any babies tonight?" said a tall gangly man as he came around the side of a hydrangea bush and started up the steps.

"Hello there, Raymond. Come and sit awhile. And you know very well, I haven't done any obstetrics for eight years or more. Your brother's daughter's youngest was the last, though peace knows I did enough in my time."

"Evening, ladies," the man named Raymond said, shuffling his straw hat and the package wrapped in brown paper from hand to hand and bowing slightly. "Aunt Mercy, Miss Booshie, Miss . . ."

"This is Henley," said Aunt Mercy, getting up and dragging another rocker from across the porch. "This is Patti's daughter. You remember Patti—one . . ."

"Mercy-my, it's hard to keep track of all those nieces of yours. More nieces than Carter has liver pills, as Mama used to say. But no, I can't remember any Patti. Whose daughter was she, anyway?"

"Yellow dress yellow dress," said Booshie, pumping the porch swing with her legs.

"What's that, Raymond? What's in that package you're worrying like a dog with a bone?" Aunt Mercy said. "Would you like some iced tea? It's warm for so early in June, and they say there are signs of a drought. Say that the farmers are feeling the pinch already. I was out at Billy Parson's place today and . . ."

"You're turning into a regular magpie tonight, Miss Mercy-my. Is that what your being here does, Henley? Turn the doctor into a chatterbox?" And Raymond sent his straw hat sailing to the other end of the porch, landing it neatly on the point of a rocking chair. "Now, about this package. I came across it this afternoon. Something you were asking after."

"Oh, Raymond, you found the book. I *am* pleased. Next time I won't be so reckless with my clearing out."

I watched as Aunt Mercy unwrapped the package and let the paper fall to the floor and then, with a kind of reverence, held the book up against the side of her face as if in some way she was listening to what it had to say. And I remembered how I had stood by the side of the road way back a hundred years ago that very morning and told Patti that I would not leave my books.

It was as if Aunt Mercy knew that, too. Only she couldn't have, because she hadn't been there. It had just been between Patti and me.

"Here, Henley," she said, holding the book out to me. "I think you'll understand. This book belonged to my mother—it was a prize she won. Earlier this spring, in a fit of trying to win out over my possessions, this somehow got bundled into the things I was sending along to Raymond for his shop. He was good enough to sort through and find it for me."

I took the book and turned it around in my hands, fingering the faded blue cover patterned with scrolls of leaves, flowers, and lutes. I touched the title, *Andersen's Fairy Tales*, in gold on the spine of the book, and the frayed edges of the binding. Opening the cover, I tipped the brittle yellow pages back in and read the certificate pasted on the inside cover, its ink now a watery brown.

YOUNG LADIES SEMINARY
Richmond, Virginia
The Second Premium
in the third class
for
General Studies
awarded to
MISS MARY PARKES WILSON
June 14th, 1892

And right away I figured that the stern-faced woman in the shadowbox frame on Aunt Mercy's wall was Mary Parkes Wilson. It gave me a funny kind of feeling to be holding her book. I turned the pages very carefully, past drawings of the Little Mermaid and Thumbelina and the Swineherd, smelling the dark musty smell. Then, as Aunt Mercy had done before me, I held the book up to my cheek.

"Raymond and his brother have a store, on a ways downtown," Aunt Mercy said. "The block past the bank, next to Shirley's Beauty Parlor, across from the railroad yard. Antiques and whatnots, and secondhand goods. Books and postcards and magazines from way back."

"Lot of junk, mostly," said Raymond, pushing his thumbs down over his belt and rocking back. "Lots of everybody's past. Yes, ma'am, after a while a little bit of everybody in town comes my way—somehow or other. Estate sales, attic cleanings, what-have-you. Guess you could say there's a history lesson right there in Fitchett

Brothers' Second-Hand. You drop on in when you get a chance, Miss Henley." Raymond stood up, leaning off the porch and looking up at the sky. "You're probably right, Miss Mercy-my, drought's taking hold." He paused. "It's a funny thing, my not remembering Patti, though."

"Twenty-five hundred and one . . ." said Booshie from her place on the swing.

After Raymond left, Aunt Mercy picked up her book and went inside. In a minute the light from the parlor splotched out onto the porch floor. She began to play the piano, the chords pulsing one after another, through the hall and out the open door onto the porch, the music seeming to come in great big gulps to swallow up the night sounds.

Booshie rocked gently in the swing and I stayed where I was, trying to fit the puzzle pieces of Aunt Mercy together.

After a while I went into the house and stood leaning on the doorjamb, feeling the vibrations from within the wood, watching Aunt Mercy, with her straight back and her fingers coming down firmly on the keys.

"Playing Chopin helps me get in touch with my feelings," she said, without turning around. The music kept right on going. Chord after throbbing chord.

Aunt Mercy was certainly getting in touch.

And so was I. Getting in touch more than I wanted to, and I yelled right out loud, "What am I doing here? Patti and I? And how come you're just letting us be, like it was okay?"

The music stopped.

"I guess in a way it is," Aunt Mercy said, starting to

play again, but this time something light and trebly. "It was important for Patti—coming here right now." There followed one good solid chord.

I clutched the doorframe and said, "Patti always used to talk about you. About being here—and what it was like. Bedtime stories, sort of."

"Aunt Mercy stories." Another chord.

"It's all because the sky was falling that we came. Only, I don't know, this place and the way Patti is . . . It doesn't seem like it's going to help."

"It's like milk toast," Aunt Mercy said. Chord. "It doesn't taste very good, but it's warm and it makes us feel good when we hurt. And right now Patti hurts. The way at times we all hurt."

There I was, all snuffled up with milk toast and the idea of hurting and the hurting itself, and Aunt Mercy knowing all about it. I clamped my hands over my ears as hard as I could and said, "I don't hurt at all, and Patti's not anemic either." Then I ran out of the room and up the stairs.

twelve

When I woke up the next morning, I was in a tangle of covers on the floor across from the bed. I blinked, trying to sit up and unwind the sheet wrapped around my knees. Something was poking me in the back, and I reached behind, feeling a step, and then another one. Looking up and over my shoulder, I saw a tall, narrow door fastened with a latch. I shook my head and pushed my way up onto the steps.

With my back pressed hard against the door, I was able to look around. The room was small, perched at the very front of the house, looking out over the green-slanted roof, then onto the street, and the houses on the other side. The door to the hall was ajar, the way I had left it the night before, and all my belongings were heaped together on the floor. There was a bed under the window, and an old treadle sewing machine draped with a flowered, gathered skirt, and a chest of drawers. And there was the door to the attic, closed with a latch that didn't look at all strong enough to hold back whatever it was that lurked on the other side.

Then I remembered why I was there—bunched together like a heap of laundry in front of the door. I had heard noises during the night: great swooping thumping noises and small scurrying sounds that sent a showering of plaster down the inside of the walls. I remembered lying in bed with the covers pulled up under my chin and my legs stretched out so straight they were numb. After a while I had turned the light on and taken out my new journal and tried to put down about Aunt Mercy and Booshie and Raymond, and everything that happened the night before. Mostly I thought about Aunt Mercy. I had always thought of her as someone from a fairy tale and not a real person with sides going all the way around. I thought about the music she played and how it made me feel happy and sad both at the same time. Then I heard the swooping noise again and had dropped the notebook and sent the pen clattering across the floor. I was going to creep into Patti's room and climb in bed with her, the way I'd done when I was small, but the long dark hall reaching down the middle of the second floor was worse than what was on the other side of the door. Finally I had dragged the covers off the bed, bundling them around me as I sat on the steps in front of the attic door, leaning against it with all my might, waiting, and watching, and sleeping some, until morning came.

"What on earth are you doing there?" Aunt Mercy said as she knocked and opened the door at the same time.

Aunt Mercy seemed to have grown since the night before. It was as though, like Alice after she ate the cake, she had become suddenly long and narrow—her short white hair brushing against the ceiling, her leather moccasins planted firmly on the floor. I saw her looming over me, only she wasn't any taller than I was, and I struggled to get up, standing on the step and pushing myself tall against the attic door.

"Well," Aunt Mercy said, picking the pillow up off the floor and tossing it on the bed. "We'll get an early start today. As soon as breakfast is over, I'll just take Patti on up the road to the hospital. While your mother is getting her blood tested, I'll stop in and see old Miss Birdy. Her fever was up again last night. Meanwhile, you and Booshie can walk down to the office so that you can see where it is. Then, while Booshie tidies up for me, you can go off and explore the town, maybe go down to the beach. Office hours start at 8:30."

"What time is it now?" I said, wondering who Miss Birdy was.

"Just after six," Aunt Mercy said.

"In the morning?" I wrapped the sheet around me like a shroud.

"Miss Birdy was the butter-and-egg lady, from long before I came to town," Aunt Mercy said, her eyes skimming the room as if picking up thoughts I might have left scattered there the night before. "I'll tell you what," she said. "Let's go and explore the garret. It's been sadly neglected lately, given over to spiders and silverfish and an occasional field mouse. Watch your step now."

I found myself hobbling up the steep, narrow attic steps behind Aunt Mercy, turning where the steps angled sharply, and climbing up to the wide-board floor. The air that pushed down at me was hot and smelled of dust. Pale, streaky light from the windows at either end barely reached the center of the attic, and I stood still while Aunt Mercy disappeared into the shadows.

"There, that's better," she said, turning on the light. She pushed at an umbrella stand with her foot and pointed to the white splotches on the floor. "Watch where you walk. Every so often, a bird gets trapped inside, gets in and can't get out. They beat themselves to death against the walls."

I shuddered and pulled the sheet tighter around me.

"Years ago, when the nieces used to come in the summertime . . ." Aunt Mercy ducked under the rafters and disappeared back into the eaves, her voice fading so that I had to follow her to hear the rest. "They used to come up here, dressing up and putting on shows. Rummaging about." She flapped at cobwebs with her hands. She bent over and eased an old trunk out of a cubbyhole. "There may be more coming at the end of the summer—the next generation—great-nieces, for their first trip East. Maybe you can bring them up here and show them all the treasures."

Before I even had a chance to think about my still being here by the end of the summer, the idea of actually being a living, breathing piece of the Aunt Mercy stories,

133

Aunt Mercy had moved on, lifting the lid of the trunk and poking at the top layer of clothes. "Barbara's wedding dress is here someplace, and Laura's jodhpurs, and the yellow sweater Sarah had before the grasshoppers got to it. And the skirt Alice tried to make one whole summer but never finished."

She moved farther into the shadows, her reflection short and squat as she passed a mirror leaning against the wall, and stopped at a stack of books and old magazines. "I thought I cleared most of this stuff out. I gave boxloads to Raymond for the store. It must multiply behind my back."

I followed Aunt Mercy to the other side of the attic, holding lightly to the trail of words as I heard about Emily, who raised guppies, and Katherine, who had collected bottle caps years ago.

When Aunt Mercy stopped to look at a bulging scrapbook, I wandered on to the farthest corner of the attic behind the steps. I fingered shoe trees and bootjacks and a jumble of wooden picture frames, and recited a litany of names under my breath. Barbara . . . Laura . . . Alice . . . Emily . . . Katherine . . . Sarah. What about Patti? Where were Patti's things? The pieces of the times when Patti came to stay? I wanted to know but was afraid to ask.

I saw a hodgepodge of old vases, urns, and gawky-looking wicker baskets with metal liners inside and wilted bow ribbons drooping from the handles. They looked like funeral baskets and I remembered the time in fourth grade when the principal's mother died and our teacher took us all along to the funeral home, which was all smarmy with the smell of flowers, and we had looked down at our shoes and poked at one another until we got outside.

All of a sudden Aunt Mercy was standing there beside me with a feather boa wrapped around her neck, looking down at the baskets, saying, "They're from Dr. John's funeral, though I can't for the life of me figure why I've kept them. It's the remembering that counts. And what's gone before. And what's to come. Because, for my own part, I believe it doesn't end. That this is just a preparation —a getting ready—for something else."

It was as though she had forgotten I was there, the way she was sitting there twirling the ends of the boa. "I think it's all a kind of interaction. Not just the way we're involved here and now with one another, but even from world to world. Nobody can convince me that my John doesn't know what's happening to me now, that he doesn't know I've gone on to do what we decided I would do."

It was weird. I mean, here I was standing in some bird-mess attic with Aunt Mercy, whom I didn't know at all, and listening to her talk out loud about some of the things I had wondered about and never been able to say.

Patti was the kind who looked the other way when a hearse went by on the street.

I wandered back across the attic, still wrapped in a sheet like an unraveling mummy, and went over to the window. I lifted the top of a tall wooden victrola and spun the turntable with my finger. "I've seen pictures, but never a real one," I said.

"It still works," said Aunt Mercy, coming up in back of me and cranking the handle. "The records are stored

135

underneath. I think Booshie comes up to listen to them, though it's the winding up she likes as much as the listening."

I closed my eyes and saw funny old lumpy Booshie turning the handle round and round, while birds swooped and soared around her and spiders dangled from the rafters in silvery webs.

"Why does she do that? I mean, why does she like to turn things and rock and rub at things over and over the way she does her hands?"

Aunt Mercy sat down on a faded red-velvet piano stool, spinning it around until her feet touched the floor. She motioned for me to sit on a wooden box beside her.

"About Booshie . . ." she said, and then waited for a long time before going on. "From what I understand, when Booshie was born, when she was very small, she was just like the rest of us, as far as anyone seems to remember. But then, when she was around three, she was lost in the woods. Her parents had gone on a trip and had taken her along. Somehow she wandered off and was lost for all of one whole night and on toward noon of the next day. She was never really the same after that."

I shivered and moved my box into the light from the window. "But how come—I mean, other people get lost— have stuff happen?"

Aunt Mercy leaned forward, resting her elbows on her knees. "That's something that no one really understands. Why someone like Booshie stays caught in a thing like that, instead of passing through it to the other side—and being stronger for that passing. I think, though I can't be sure, that there's a logic to the way she leads her life. The things she does are her way of protecting herself against the terrors all around her."

Aunt Mercy got up and took a record out of the cabinet under the victrola. She put it on the turntable and set the needle down on the record. A thin, wavery music filled the attic. "The last time I saw Paris, her streets were young and gay . . ."

"This was one of my mother's old records, one of the ones the girls used to like to play when they came home. The victrola was in the library then and the house was always filled with music. When the family was here—Booshie and the nieces, my sisters and brothers and the sisters- and brothers-in-law, the times as Patti remembers them—"

"Booshie's not your family," I said, and my voice slammed back at me from the rafters overhead.

The record came to an end and continued going around.

Aunt Mercy didn't say anything.

I clutched my sheet and headed for the steps, feeling suddenly that I had gone too far.

Behind me, the needle scratched against the record. I heard Aunt Mercy lift it off, stop the machine, and lower the lid. Her voice was steely quiet. "To my way of thinking, she is. According to the Psalms, 'God setteth the solitary in families,' and it's hard to think of anyone much more solitary than Booshie was."

Aunt Mercy's words seemed to wrap around me like the feather boa that she was putting over the shoulders of a dressmaker's dummy. And the attic in back of me, hot, and jumbled, looked wonderfully safe, as if everything was the way it ought to be.

When I got down to breakfast, Patti was already there. Her face looked softened, almost smudged, and she greeted me as if I were somebody she didn't know very well. Sitting down next to her, I poked her under the table and rolled my eyes when Booshie came in from the pantry counting out loud. Patti looked back at me blankly.

Then I got this really scary feeling that Patti had just given herself up to Aunt Mercy and let her do something to her brain. That Aunt Mercy gave her some awful evil potion to make her not be like Patti anymore.

"Maybe she's a witch—a sorcerer," I thought, warming to the story. "Maybe she's an enchantress and she did this to Booshie and now she's going to do it to Patti and me."

Then I remembered the okay parts of Aunt Mercy: how she led me through the attic until I wasn't scared anymore, and sometimes seemed to know the way I was thinking.

Then I didn't know what to think about anything at all.

After breakfast, Aunt Mercy hurried us outside, opening the car door for Patti and pointing me in the direction of town, along with Booshie, who stood ready to go like a wind-up toy waiting for someone to release the spring. I kept expecting Patti to tell me to get in the car and come along. Waiting for her to turn the trip to the hospital with Aunt Mercy into a joke, or an expedition.

But she didn't, and the next thing I knew, the car was gone and I was following Booshie down the street. I mean, it was better than walking next to her, and I didn't have the nerve not to go at all. I stared at Booshie's back: the tufts of hair and the baggy, flowered dress with its crooked hem, the blue-white legs, the arms held stiffly out on either side as if keeping her in balance.

Squuunching up my eyes, I stuck my tongue out as far as it would go and waggled it sideways until my mouth was dry and my whole face ached. I dragged my feet, kicking at sticks and leaf pods and stones, then switched to carefully measured heel-toe steps, inching my way along the sidewalk. Booshie still stumped out in front of me, and when she got to every corner she waited, without turning around, for me to catch up—so we could cross together. Once we were on the other side, I dropped back again and Booshie shambled on ahead, until she got to the next corner.

I tripped on a bump in the sidewalk and caught myself just before I went sprawling forward. I bit my tongue and felt a sudden prickling of tears behind my eyes.

We crossed the street and went past the library and the Presbyterian church. We passed a funny ragtag woman pulling a wagon down the middle of the street, followed by a girl about my age. When Booshie stopped and seemed to be talking to the woman in that funny flappy way that wasn't really talking at all, I stopped too, marking time by poking at a clump of grass growing up between the cracks of the sidewalk. The girl was staring at me and looking as if maybe she was going to say something, but I turned my back and poked harder at the bunch of grass, wishing that she would and wouldn't, both at the same time. Suddenly the girl lurched forward, grabbing hold of the wagon by the handle and pulling it away, calling back over her shoulder, "Come on, Gussie. Last one there's a rotten egg."

When the girl and the woman she called Gussie turned

up a side street and disappeared, Booshie and I went on. Then, without even thinking about it, I ran ahead, dodging past Booshie, cutting up onto the grass and darting over lawns and on to the corner. But once I was there, something held me back. I turned and waited for Booshie to catch up so we could cross the street together.

thirteen

When we got to Aunt Mercy's office, Booshie rooted in her pocket for her bunch of keys, opening the door and pushing me into the waiting room ahead of her. The smell of medicine caught at me, surprised me. I mean, I had always known Aunt Mercy was a doctor. I had seen her black doctor bag and knew that she had ordered blood tests done on Patti at the hospital this morning. But even that didn't make me realize it as much as seeing that office did. I stood in the doorway between the waiting room and the inner office and looked at the examining table, the scale, the glass-fronted cabinet with gauze and tape and cotton inside, at the tongue depressors and lollipops. I thought about how I started to put Aunt Mercy together the day before from her room at home; how I was seeing another part of her; and how maybe we're all made up of the things we leave around us. I looked at the great huge battered desk and the great huge chair and thought how Aunt Mercy would disappear in all that hugeness. Then I walked around the side of the desk and saw that the "R" and "S" volumes of the *Encyclopaedia Britannica* were piled up there for her to sit on, and I knew right away that Aunt Mercy would never be swallowed up at all.

I went out of the office, through the waiting room, to the outside, wondering what I was supposed to do next. Aunt Mercy said, "See the office," and I had seen it. She said, "See the town," and as far as I could tell, I'd seen that too. Should I go, or wait, or what?

I stood for a few minutes and watched Booshie sweep the sidewalk. As she worked her way first in one direction and then back the way she had come, the broom made a scratching noise against the cement. People passing by had to move onto the grass or into the street to keep from being swept away. I had the feeling that these same people had been stepping around Booshie sweeping the same sidewalk forever.

A woman carrying a baby in one of those papoose things went into the waiting room. Then other patients came like a parade: a man with a cane, and another man with a bandage on his arm; a woman dragging twins, and an old lady in a yellow hat. The waiting room started to fill up, and I thought about all those people hoping for Aunt Mercy to cure them with her pills and potions and lollipops. After that, my imagination just kept right on going and there was Aunt Mercy back in the fourteenth century treating the black plague then off on an island somewhere with the lepers.

142

I heard a car door slam and opened my eyes in time to see Aunt Mercy herself coming along, carrying her doctor bag in one hand and a McDonald's milk shake in the other. She put her arm around Booshie, breaking the pattern of her sweeping. "That's fine, Booshie. But come on now, there are things for you to do inside. Oh, Henley," she said, looking at me. "Patti's fine. The test they did at the lab this morning was normal. I dropped her at the house so she could get something to eat, and I'm sure, given a bit more rest, she'll be feeling like herself again." She started toward the door, then stopped. "If you turn at the corner and go straight down Main Street, you'll come to the bay. Maybe later you and Patti might want to swim."

So much for the black plague.

I stood on the sidewalk and felt dismissed. For a minute I thought about going home and fixing breakfast for Patti or finding the beach or trying out the library. But there was something I had to do first.

I turned onto Main Street and went past Trimper's Dry-Goods Store, past the drugstore and the Palace movie theater. I stopped for a minute in front of the Pop Shop and stared through the window at the popcorn machine and smelled the hot butter and watched the fan turning lazily from the ceiling. Then I went on, looking up at the store fronts.

"Fitchett Brothers' Second-Hand," Raymond had said the night before. "Lots of everybody's past."

". . . the block past the bank, next to Shirley's Beauty Parlor, across from the railroad yard . . ." Aunt Mercy had said.

From somewhere up ahead and across the street, a

freight train screeched and clattered as it was shunted onto another siding.

I started to run.

It was more like a barn than a store, with its double doors propped open by a Franklin stove on one side and an old rocking horse on the other. The grass in front was scuffed and there were two tires painted white, piled high with conch shells. A rickety table heaped with a jumble of used toasters, irons, and electrical cords stood under the sign, faded red on white, hanging overhead: FITCHETT BROTHERS' SECOND-HAND.

"Morning, Henley," said Raymond, coming to stand in the doorway. "Glad you came by. This is George, the other half of Fitchett Brothers' Second-Hand. The better half, I always say." And he laughed and slapped the side of his leg and nodded to the man coming around the side of an old refrigerator in back of him.

"It's a funny thing," Raymond went on. "My not remembering which one of the nieces Patti was. Couldn't remember last night, and truth to tell, I can't remember this morning either. Neither can George. I asked him when I got home."

"We're not the Fitchetts with the memory, though," said George.

"That's Mama he's talking about. If Mama was with us now, she'd know for sure. Never forgot a thing."

"Time the ladies of the Baptist church were getting a history together, not one of them could recall the year the old church burned."

"Had to come ask Mama, and she set them right," Raymond said. "It was 1924."

" '25," said George.

" '24. I know because I was in the second grade and you were in the third."

"I wasn't in the third grade in 1924."

"It's right there in black and white. Based on Mama's rememberings . . ."

"Well, we'll see about that," said George, hurrying to the back of the store. "There's a copy of that book here somewhere. Soon as I put my hand on it . . ."

"We'll see. We'll just see," said Raymond, settling down on a bench to wait.

I slipped away and started down the first aisle. As I rummaged through a box of old postcards, my eyes skimmed messages and paused briefly at signatures. I took books off shelves, looking for ones that might have come from Aunt Mercy's attic, that might have been read by Patti. At the back wall I stepped over a pile of duck decoys and started down the next aisle, riffling old magazines and pawing through a collection of dress patterns as if I expected to see Patti posing on the cover of a Simplicity envelope.

At the front of the store, Raymond was dozing in the sun, his head nodding back and forth, but just as I turned into the next aisle, he spoke to me. "That Aunt Mercy of yours is quite a woman. Quite a person, I'd say. It was back around the late thirties that she first came to town as Dr. John's bride. Wasn't long before he took sick, though. And all the time through that sickness—right up until he died—they talked and figured and planned how Mercy would go on to medical school after he was gone, and then come back and take his place."

I stood there swaying beside a big, old-fashioned plant stand, my fingers tracing the raised china bows and curlicues, my feet barely still. Part of me wanted to continue my search; part wanted to stay and hear about Aunt Mercy.

"Is that what she did? Go to school after he died? Dr. John, I mean."

"Bless pat, she did. Went right down to the Medical College of Georgia. Graduated, too, and came back here and opened up her office."

"And everybody was glad," I said, much in the way I like to put "And they lived happily ever after" endings on the stories I write.

"Not a bit of it," said Raymond, leaning forward and filling his pipe. "Never had a woman doctor in town before, and folks didn't quite know what to make of it. Then one day Jessie Wilkins's German shepherd tore his leg on a piece of barb wire and Jessie took him over to Mercy's brand-new office, right where it is now. Never knew whether he did it for pure devilment or not, but Mercy, she just sewed that dog's leg on up and everybody waited and the dog got well and since then there's scarcely been an empty chair in her waiting room. Human beings, that is."

And then the Madame Curie part of Aunt Mercy seemed to take over again and I could just see her there being nobler than life and taking care of somebody's dog and waiting for real people to come along.

Raymond pulled me up short. "You know something, Miss Henley. I think my mama hoped that . . . well, after

Dr. John died and all . . . after Miss Mercy came back, that she and I . . . well, you know, that maybe we might . . . And truth to tell, it wasn't just Mama had that idea . . . I thought right kindly of it myself. Took to going round there of an evening now and then, but there never seemed to be a chance . . . the right words never seemed to come."

I waited, but when Raymond didn't say anymore, I moved along, sorting through sheet music and records that were heavy and brittle, and china dogs and empty picture frames. All the time I was looking, I thought about what Raymond had said and thought of him coming around the night before, and wondered how many nights through the years he had come along like that.

"Always one to do for somebody else," Raymond called from his place on the bench. "That's her way. Like taking Miss Booshie in after her mother and father up and died one after the other. To keep her from being sent away."

I thought back to what I had said in Aunt Mercy's attic and it was like touching a bruise.

Flipping through a cardboard box of old photographs, I stopped suddenly, then worked my way backward and held up a picture of a group of girls and boys on the beach. I put a circle of my fingers around one of the girls, holding the picture close, then far away. I squinted at it, tilting it into the light, then back into the shadows. As much as I wanted her to be, she wasn't Patti. I slammed the picture back into the box and turned to see Booshie watching me, nodding and swaying and counting under her breath.

Booshie didn't say anything. She didn't reach out and touch the books or finger the gewgaws piled in orange crates or cardboard boxes. She didn't pay any attention to the mangy fringed shawl hanging from a nail or the china shepherd chasing a china shepherdess.

She followed me. Hovering. Staying just beside me.

"Eighty thousand six hundred and four . . . eighty thousand six . . ."

I tried to turn away: to veer from one side of the aisle to the other, but Booshie was right there. Her nearness pushed like a spider web against my face.

Raymond spoke from the edges of his nap. "Morning, Miss Booshie. It's been a long time since you've been down here to see us."

"She hasn't been here for a powerful long time," he said, turning to me. "Must be something special to bring her along this way."

"Eighty thousand six hundred and thirty-six . . ." said Booshie.

When we were out on the sidewalk, Booshie turned and headed back the way she had come, toward Aunt Mercy's office, still without saying anything except for that dumb counting. I stood for a minute watching her, then I turned and went the other way, past the television repair shop and the Crown Dry-cleaners. I crossed the street and went alongside the vacant field, where tough stalky sea grass grew in clumps and the sidewalk was gritty with sand. A banner, hanging between two utility poles, flapped overhead, and I stepped back, craning my neck to read about the Firemen's Carnival that was "Coming Soon. July 4–6." Then I ran across the street and up the slope.

Sitting on the edge of the boardwalk, I kicked off my shoes and dug my feet down into the sand, past the surface hot part and on into where it was cool. The bay was flat and still, the tide was low, and the sandbar, patterned with ripples, stretched and sprawled out in front of me. A group of kids were playing by the edge of the water and a fat white sea gull skimmed the beach. I sat with my face held up to the sun and thought about things. About how Aunt Mercy had said that Patti was okay and would soon be her regular self. I was glad about that. And how living with Patti got to be scary sometimes because I wasn't always sure how long she could hold on to whatever it was she was trying to hold on to. Or how long I could hold on to her. Or even exactly what it was about Patti that I couldn't understand. I was her kid, for pete's sake.

When I didn't like thinking about that anymore, I thought about not finding any of Patti's past at Raymond's store and about Booshie coming along before I really had a chance to look, about the sky falling, and finally being at Aunt Mercy's, and whether things were really going to be different anyway.

Then I thought about Raymond. And what he had said about Aunt Mercy. That seemed an okay thing to think about, but weird. I mean, Raymond and Aunt Mercy—like *that*? Then I thought about how there couldn't have been any of that because of Raymond saying he just kept going round to call—year after year—and how he could never speak up. Maybe he should have had a spokesman, a John Alden, sort of.

I slid off the boardwalk onto the sand and scrunched back against a piling and thought about how Raymond wasn't exactly a romantic figure, with his little bit of a potbelly and those splotchy brown spots on his hands. And old. But I guess he hadn't always been. Or Aunt Mercy, either. I tried to think what they must have looked like young, about the time Aunt Mercy came back to town from the Medical College of Georgia. A young widow. Alone. And everybody not sure she would be a good doctor because she was a woman. And Raymond going round to call. Young. Silent. But loving her and sticking up for her, and, when she cured Jessie Wilkins's dog, I could just see Raymond going all around town saying, "I told you so. I told you so."

Then I worked out a 1–2–3 plan in my head about why nothing ever came of it. *One* was, maybe Aunt Mercy had been so dedicated, promising Dr. John before he died that she would carry on with his work. There wasn't time for anything else.

Number 2 was, Raymond just never spoke up. That Aunt Mercy never knew.

Number 3 had to do with Raymond's saying it was all his mama's idea; how maybe that turned Aunt Mercy off. Aunt Mercy seemed like a pretty tough person, and Raymond might not have been tough enough. Not that I liked to think he was a wimp exactly, except I do tend to think people should be able to do things on their own.

One. Two. Three. Out of these, I went with number 2: Raymond never being able to tell Aunt Mercy how he felt; she never knew. Then I started thinking that it might not be too late now. Maybe they weren't really all that old. Maybe it didn't make any difference.

All of a sudden I felt sad. And lonely. I didn't want

to feel that way, so I brushed my feet off and put on my shoes, knowing I just had to *do* something.

I looked down the length of the boardwalk, through the gazebo that straddled it halfway along, and out the other side to the old fishing pier. I started forward, making giant steps on the boards. "I bet that's as far as the town goes on this end," I thought, looking toward the pier. "And Main Street on the one side, and where Aunt Mercy lives is almost at the top, and whatever else is over there." I had a sudden sense of boundaries. The giant steps turned into a jog, then to a run as I raced along, up the step and through the gazebo and down again. Past the beach scattered with shells, driftwood, and tangled seaweed on one side and houses lined across the street on the other. I ran the six blocks to the pier, not thinking at all. Just running, running, running. Then I turned and, dropping back to a jog, went back the way I had come, until I got to Aunt Mercy's street. I turned up Mulberry Street, walking now—but with the feel of running—and headed home, anxious to find Patti: to tell her that it was okay for us to be here.

Patti was lying on a yellow bedspread in Aunt Mercy's back yard, her eyes closed, her face pointed toward the sun.

"Come on, Patti," I said, flopping on the corner of the spread. "Come on. I found the beach and we can go as soon as I get my bathing suit on. I'll pack a lunch and this afternoon when the tide comes in we can swim and . . ."

Patti sat up, reaching for her sunglasses and putting them on. "My God—have you seen the beach? It's pathetic. Dinky and puny. I mean, the whole damn town's no wider than the boardwalk. Besides, bay water's murky. And there are sea nettles. There's nothing there. I mean, it's not exactly Atlantic City."

Sunspots swirled before my eyes and I looked down at the spread and plaited the fringe into tight stubby braids. And didn't say anything.

Patti poured baby oil into her hand and smoothed it on her legs. "Now there's a thought, Henny-penny. Atlantic City. You've never been to Atlantic City, and now that the casinos are there, maybe we should think about it."

fourteen

It was summertime and I woke every morning to the
smack of heat that seemed to carry over from the night
before. I woke to damp pillows and my hair stuck to the
side of my head; the cord of the window shade that hung
in front of the open window and never stirred, and the
sound of the early-morning ringing of the telephone.

"Good God, it's like being caught in a trap—every day
just like the one before," Patti would say over and over,
with her face pressed against the screen door, looking like
the picture of the lion with the silver-colored bars across the
glass in Aunt Mercy's dining room.

In the mornings I would lie in bed and study the room
around me: the attic door and the dresser and the picture
that hung over the sewing machine of a curly-haired girl

feeding a carrot to a rabbit. My books were there—in the bookcase that Aunt Mercy had helped me drag down from the attic. My carved wooden box was on the window-sill, and a duck made of overlapping shells that one of the nieces had left behind.

"Junk," Patti said, looking in the door one day. "Tacky, secondhand junk. That's what comes of letting your taste be formed by hanging around Fitchett Brothers' Second-Hand. Honestly, sweetie, it's junk."

I would wait until I heard Aunt Mercy go downstairs, then I would get up, pulling on my shirt and shorts, and go down the hall to the bathroom, which was the size of a regular room and tiled all around with big square flat tiles that sometimes had Aunt Mercy's handkerchiefs sticking to them where she flattened them to dry after she washed them out. There was a loosened brown tile on the floor that clanked when I stepped on it, and a bathtub on feet, with a splotch of rust underneath the spigot. There was a window looking out onto the back yard, and yellow dotted-swiss curtains that were stiff and scratchy. And there was an enormous mirror on the wall opposite the tub that had ripples in the glass and made me look sturdy and stolid and not at all the way I wanted to look.

"I've got to get out of here," Patti would say, slamming out of the bathroom. "Not even a shower. It's a wonder you don't have to use an outhouse in the yard."

154

I went through the gate at the end of the hall and down the narrow, twisting back stairs, holding my breath after the last turn as I stood in the pocket of darkness and groped down low for the knob of the kitchen door. Then I would burst out into the kitchen, where Aunt Mercy stood at the stove and Booshie shuffled back and forth between the table and the pantry, nodding and counting under her breath.

The three of us would sit at the breakfast table.

"I could use you down at the office today, Booshie," Aunt Mercy would say sometimes.

Or, "I'm not going to need you today. You might want to work on your flower bed."

"And, Henley, if you go by the Pop Shop, be sure and pick up a city paper."

Or, "The farmers are desperate for rain . . ."

"There was an earthquake in California. I heard it on the news . . ."

And Booshie would say, "Three thousand and six . . ." or, "Seventeen thousand and twenty-four . . ." depending on where she was in her counting at the moment.

"I'm going to Raymond's," or "the beach," or "to explore," I said.

"I saw that girl again, the one with the old woman and the wagon," I said once.

"Her name is Slug, and Gussie is her grandmother," Aunt Mercy said.

"H, my name is Henley," I thought.

"One thousand and one . . ." said Booshie.

Just as we were finishing up, Patti would rush into the

kitchen and drink a cup of coffee, going out without saying anything to the rest of us. Aunt Mercy had gotten her a job in the office of the Light and Power Company downtown, next to Trimper's Dry-Goods Store.

"Don't follow me," Patti said when I started off to walk her to work the first few days. "Don't—follow—me. Don't push at me all the time, making sure I get to work like a good little girl. Patti-do-this: Patti-do-that. I took the goddamn job. What more do you want from me?"

Sometimes in the morning I went to Fitchett Brothers' Second-Hand and sat on the bench, talking to Raymond and his brother George, listening to the stories about Mama and George's dead wife and his children and his children's children. Sometimes I would even help Raymond unpack the things he bought at sales, and put the books on shelves, the lamps and sheet music and crocheted antimacassars on display.

I had watched Raymond and Aunt Mercy a lot and had pretty much decided that their story wasn't a very exciting one. Mostly I think because Raymond talked about Mama an awful lot, and there he was, a grown-up old man. And besides, Mama had been dead for ages. But there were things about Raymond and the way he felt about Aunt Mercy that I couldn't let go, so I had lumped all these things into another story about this sort of old man named Harold and this really nice woman named Susan who went off somewhere to be a missionary even after Harold begged her to stay home and then the headhunters got her. Actually, I wasn't sure about the headhunter part. In fact,

I kept changing the ending, in my head and then on paper in my notebook. Anyhow, that way I felt that even if Raymond and Aunt Mercy didn't really love each other, the story wasn't wasted.

Sometimes I would go to the beach, sitting on the sand by myself and staring at the water, or climbing out on the jetty, the rocks warm against my feet, the water sloshing beneath me. When the tide was low, I would walk out onto the sandbar, past the periwinkles, into the lukewarm water that slapped my legs, looking for jellyfish and seaweed and feeling the gritty firmness of the bottom underfoot. And sometimes—thinking about this makes me feel crawly— when the kids who were there would rush past me, pushing out to the deeper water, swarming onto the wooden platform and up the ladder covered with barnacles and green slime, I would swim around the edges of them. That way I could pretend to myself that I was a part of them. But not a part. Maybe what I really hoped would happen was that in all that pushing and splashing I would just get bunched along with them into a game of tag. But it never did.

I wasn't the only one swimming around on the edge of things, though. Sometimes the girl named Slug would be there, diving and floating and swimming underwater. The same as I was doing, only we were doing it apart together. Neither one of us saying anything at all. On those days when Slug was there, I would see her grandmother Gussie trundling that funny red wagon of hers up and down the beach, or just settling herself down on the hot dry sand to watch the sky.

Anyway, after a while Gussie would come down to the water's edge, waving her arms, and Slug would go running into shore, her knees and elbows going in all directions and setting up a great surge of water around her. She would throw a towel around her shoulders, and the two of them would go along. After she left, I always had an empty feeling inside of me that I had to be careful about.

I would do Aunt Mercy's errands for her, stopping to talk to Mr. Brown on the corner by the bank, picking up bread at the store, and nodding to the people who were beginning to fill in the spaces around me. When I passed the store-front office of the Light and Power Company, I could see Patti slouching onto the counter, looking at the clock on the wall in back of her.

"Did anybody call?" Patti would ask, getting me aside when she came in for lunch. "I called Angel from work and left word for her to call me back. I've got to get out of here."

Sometimes in the afternoon I would go with Aunt Mercy to make a house call, riding out the old road that humped over the railroad yard and alongside the Episcopal cemetery and on past fields and patches of woods to a house by the side of the road or at the end of a rutted, dusty drive. And Aunt Mercy, perched there on a faded yellow cushion peering over the steering wheel, told me about the houses and the people in her loud clear voice.

"Miss Rose Mae Parsons lives down there. Used to be a teacher at the high school before she retired."

"That's the old Waters place, around that turn in the road . . ."

Sometimes we would go out the highway, past the giant

water tower and the Texaco station and Savages garage, up the ten miles or so to the red brick hospital, which seemed to rise out of a stretch of field. I would sit outside under a crape-myrtle tree and read a book while Aunt Mercy made her rounds.

The funny thing was that on these trips Aunt Mercy and I began to talk. To each other, I mean. It was as though we each had a stack of cards and were leaning and tilting them one against the other, hoping they would all stand up.

One day Aunt Mercy came out of the hospital and sat down on the grass next to me, waiting for me to get to the end of a chapter. "When Dr. John first came here to town, this hospital was just opening up," she said. "Before that, patients had to be taken across the bay by ferry."

"Tell me about the time you treated Jessie Wilkins's German shepherd," I said.

And Aunt Mercy leaned back on her elbows and looked up at the sky and started to laugh. "My first patient here in town. His name was Arnold, and that silly dog lived fifteen years more. I guess you've been talking to Raymond."

"Hey, Aunt Mercy, how come after Dr. John died, you never married anybody else?" The words were out before I even thought about saying them.

"Oh, now I *know* you've been talking to Raymond," she said, laughing again. But it wasn't a mean kind of laugh. "Poor dear Raymond."

And right away I knew the answer—to the Raymond part, at least. Aunt Mercy could never have married anyone she had to call "poor dear" anything.

"Besides," she went on, sitting up, "Dr. John and I were awesomely happy together."

159

She said it just that way. "Awesomely happy."

"And anyway, maybe the right person just hasn't come along," Aunt Mercy said.

Then it was my turn to laugh. Not because it was funny exactly, but maybe because it was sunny out and the ground smelled good and was covered all over with clover and Aunt Mercy seemed pretty okay. The two of us sat there and laughed with one another.

Then all of a sudden I just stopped. I pulled at the grass around me until the ground was bare, and I felt my heart thumping inside and said all in a rush that I couldn't take back, "Sometimes I'm not sure about Patti—why she's how she is and what's going to happen to us . . ."

Just then a car came racing past us with its horn blaring and gravel splattering all around and pulled up to the emergency door and a man and woman got out, carrying a hurt little boy, and Aunt Mercy ran to help.

Afterwards, when we were on the way home, I knew—and knew that Aunt Mercy knew—that the time wasn't right to get back to it. But that was okay. It was a beginning.

On days when I didn't go with Aunt Mercy, I would explore. I went to the top of Mulberry Street and followed the gully by the edge of the field, lined all along with loblolly pines, which ran across the north side of town. I saw the ragtag little houses on past Nectarine Street, and the trees that grew out of small hard plots of ground.

One day I went past the confectioner's store and crossed the street to the school, pacing off the playground. I walked around and around the building, looking up at empty windows, wondering what it would be like to go to school there.

I sat on the bottom row of bleachers and drew patterns in the dust with the toes of my tennis shoes and imagined long-ago ball games. At the other end of the bleachers I saw the girl Slug sitting, drawing pictures in the dust. I looked away, then back quickly, and away again. I moved up a row, and so did Slug. And up and up and up, until we both sat on the top row, apart from each other and staring straight ahead. "H, my name is Henley . . . H, my name is Henley, and I live in Henlopen . . ." I thought. I sat until my bottom was numb with sitting there, then I jumped down the back of the bleachers and ran away.

I walked the streets on the edge of town where the houses drifted farther apart and the sidewalks disappeared and the grass grew taller and edged closer to the gutters. I found a turtle that had been run over by a car and traced the diamonds on its back with a stick as they lay flattened on the road like a decal. I went to the library, taking two books at a time and returning two, setting up a kind of rotation so that I was never without at least two books I hadn't read.

"I can't take it much longer," Patti said again and again. "This town and the people and this house. I've got to call Eric, get hold of him . . ." I began to see the dark, pinched look on Patti's face and I was scared to see it there.

After supper, we would sit on the porch and listen to the sound of crickets and little children playing hide-and-

161

seek on the next street over, and wait for dark, and watch for fireflies.

"It's closing in on us, Henny-penny," Patti would say, resting her forehead on the pillar of the porch and holding tight until her fingers turned an angry white.

Sometimes, when I would go inside to get a drink of water or go to the bathroom, I would hear Patti talking on the telephone, her voice high-pitched and frayed, asking for Eric or Angel or Margey, then dropping to a whisper.

At night Aunt Mercy would play the piano. Booshie would sit on the swing, rocking and rubbing at her hand as though it were an injured animal. The music would come out the doors and the open windows and push through the dark and the heat and the cricket sound, so that the Tuckers on their porch across the street, and the Kellams next door, and the Ayres farther up Mulberry Street would stop their rocking and listen.

"I hate music and I hate Chopin and I hate this whole damn place," Patti would say, running upstairs and slamming the door.

I would stand by the parlor door, listening to the music, and to the sound of Patti's footsteps as she paced back and forth overhead.

fifteen

One morning early in July, I found Patti standing in the front hall long after the time she usually left for work.

"Because I didn't want to," she said before I even opened my mouth. "I didn't want to go. I didn't feel like it. I'm sick of going every day to the Light and Power Company and leaning on the counter and waiting for somebody to come in and pay a bill. Looking out the window at the world going by." She moved over next to the bust of the Indian girl on the pedestal, and her face looked twisted and angry beside the blandness of the statue's face.

Patti kept on with her one-sided conversation. "What a place. On a good day I get to see Mrs. Wilgus on her way to the store for milk. Or Jessie Penny Nottingham going to the five-and-dime. Mr. Trimper for a newspaper, or fat old Billy Parsons and his fat old dog."

"But, Patti . . ." I said.

"But Patti what? But Patti . . . but Patti . . . but Patti . . . Christ. Talk about the window of the world. I see it all. Gussie and her wagon and that tag-along kid. And you—I see you too, going along with your grocery bag, looking smug. The Coca-Cola truck comes on Thursdays, and the Sunshine Bread three days a week to the Colonial Store. The Trailways bus comes in the afternoon and goes right back out again. The driver doesn't even stop long enough for coffee. Train comes in, too. And it leaves again at night. I hear the whistle every night. At least there are ways out. I have to believe in that."

"It's only been two weeks," I said. "You've only had that job two weeks, and that's not any time at all."

"I've had it forever. And the one before that and the one before that. There's no creativity. No challenge. You're not listening to me."

And I guess Patti in a way was right. I mean, I was *listening* to her, but I wasn't *hearing* her. Mostly I kept thinking about how Aunt Mercy got her the job, and if she quit, how things just might go back to being the way they were before, and about what would happen then. "But Aunt Mercy got that job for you," I blurted out. "You can't just not go, especially when she's not here now. When she had to go out on an early call."

"The job was right there in the *County Times*. All she had to do was circle the ad. It was right on the page where it said 'Kitty Lee Dunton is convalescing at Memorial Hospital and wishes to thank her many friends for their cards and letters.' Right on the same page with Henry Lynam's gallbladder."

I stepped back against the newel post and thought how I

liked to read the personals in the *County Times*. How it made me comfortable to know that Anna Lou Taylor was resting after surgery and that Reverend Kellam spent the day in Norfolk last week. Even if I didn't know them, I felt good. Sometimes, when I was in bed at night, I worked on an item in my head that said, "The town's own Dr. Mercy has as her guests this week her niece Patti and her great-niece Henley from Baltimore. When reached for comment at her home on Mulberry Street, Dr. Mercy said, 'This visit just might go on forever.' "

Out loud I said, "But you said this time we were going to settle down. To stay."

"We did settle down," said Patti, her voice spinning higher and higher. "We stayed. We mired right on in. And you know what? It's stagnant. Dead. And if we stay here we're going to get that way too, and I'm not going to let it happen to me. We should never have come."

"But, Patti, it's . . . I mean, the house and everything. And Aunt Mercy, and Booshie and . . . I . . ."

"The house is old and dull and nothing's changed."

I pushed farther back so that the point of the newel post was digging into my shoulder.

"The house is nothing but a white elephant. Nobody cares about back stairs anymore. Or porches, and that attic. Buzzers in every room as if there were someone to answer them. Feet on the bathtub, and the same old musty smells that have always been here."

There was Patti taking all the stuff I liked and making it sound as if there were something wrong with it. "I like it," I said, but the words sounded smaller than I wanted them to sound.

"We've got to get out of here. I've been talking to Angel, to Eric, to my other friends. I *do* have friends. And you know what, Henny-penny, things are going to work out, I think. We'll make them work. The two of us."

"Did you pay Aunt Mercy for the telephone calls?" I asked, thinking about Patti huddled against the phone at night. "Long-distance costs a lot." And right away I had the feeling of being right back where we had been before, with me telling Patti the things it would be better if she already knew.

"Don't start on me about money. Don't start on me." Patti moved into a splotch of light made by the sunlight coming through the stained-glass window, her face taking on a mottled yellow look. "It wasn't much, and Aunt Mercy has money. If she doesn't, let her patients pay her in rutabagas or something. What does she have to spend her money on besides Booshie, anyway?" Then Patti broke into a lumbering kind of dance around the hall, with her head bobbing back and forth and her hands stroking one another. "Here it is—the Booshie dance." Patti shuffled around and around, muttering under her breath, "Seven hundred and one . . . seven hundred and two . . ." while I crouched back against the wall, in the corner at the foot of the stairs.

"And now, ladies and gentlemen," said Patti, stopping, then starting up again. "Now we have the Booshie sweep." She swung her imaginary broom with short rhythmic strokes. "Look at her down there," said Patti, peering out the screen door.

Flattened back in that corner, I felt a horrid black bitter taste rise up in my throat and I swallowed back against it over and over. I gagged on that taste and on the thoughts that churned inside me. Thoughts about Patti, and the things she did—crazy runaround things that kept me chasing after her because I didn't know what else to do. But now there was something else. A meanness that reached out all around me and filled the hall, making me want to fight against it as hard as I could.

Finally, I was able to move over to the door. Looking out, I saw Booshie down on the sidewalk with her broom. Sweeping steadily and slowly in her funny clumpy way.

"The Booshie sweep," cried Patti, pushing her way out the door. She pantomimed her way across the porch and down the walk. Sweeping. Sweeping. Sweeping.

I followed her slowly, in a kind of walking horror, as if the message was not getting from my eyes to my brain to my feet.

And down on the sidewalk Booshie swept faster and faster. She moved in a frenzy, saying, "Yellow dress . . . yellow dress . . . yellow dress . . ." She swept backward and forward like an animal caught in a maze. "Yellow dress . . . yellow dress . . . yellow dress . . ." Her voice rose to a wail.

"*Damn the yellow dress*," said Patti, grabbing the broom out of Booshie's hands and jumping back onto the grass.

"Yellow dress . . . yellow dress . . ." said Booshie, moving rhythmically back down the sidewalk, her arms still making sweeping motions.

I ran. "Give it back to her," I said, standing in front of Patti. "Give it back to her."

"Why should I?" she said, sweeping at the grass. "As

if I didn't know what she's already told you. All those times walking downtown together. Or when you did the dishes. As if I didn't know how she told you I don't really belong here at all. That I'm not one of the nieces. That I was just a friend of Barbara's and came with her in the summers. I don't belong here. That's why there aren't any pictures of me on the wall. Nothing of mine in the attic. Why Raymond can't remember me, only he's too simple to figure out to keep his mouth shut. The way Aunt Mercy does. The way I knew she would. Because she *is* Aunt Mercy. I don't belong here at all. And you know what, Henny-penny. If I don't belong here, then you don't belong here either."

Booshie screamed.

I wrenched the broom out of Patti's hands and ran to Booshie and held it out to her. After a while I took Booshie's fingers and curled them around the red wooden handle and helped her to sweep and tried not to see the tears that were running down her face, running down and dripping onto her dress as though they would never stop.

As Booshie began to sweep on her own, I stepped back, away from her. I saw that Patti was no longer in sight, that Aunt Mercy was moving toward me. It was as though I were watching all this from far away.

Aunt Mercy touched me on the arm and motioned me away, over under a tree. "I just got here—and saw it all," she said. "I think Booshie will be all right now. But how about you?"

That "How about you?" undid something inside me—as though all the little parts of myself were coming unhooked from all the other parts. I swayed and my knees started to buckle. Aunt Mercy caught me and put her arm around my shoulder. "Walk around back to the car with me. I have to be getting on. The waiting room is sure to be crowded by now. But there are a few minutes to talk. And lots more time later on."

I followed Aunt Mercy across the grass and down the driveway, to the place where she always parked her car, under the study windows. We stood next to the car and I made patterns on it in the dust. For a long time, we didn't say anything.

"Ever since you came, Booshie has wanted to protect you, to keep you from knowing that Patti wasn't one of my nieces. The way she let you think she was," Aunt Mercy said. "Though it wouldn't have made any difference to us after all this time. Patti came back because she needed something. But I'm not sure we've been able to give it to her. When I saw what Booshie was doing, well—maybe I shouldn't have let her do it."

Then I saw it, too. I remembered the first time I had gone to Fitchett Brothers' Second-Hand, how Booshie had come along, moving between me and the things on the shelves, to keep me away from what I would never find. I remembered Booshie moving back and forth in front of the pictures on the wall in Aunt Mercy's study, and coming along behind me all the times I had gone poking in the attic.

"What about the yellow dress?" I said.

Aunt Mercy took a breath that seemed bigger than she was. "Your mother—Patti—came from college several times with my niece Barbara. There was always a restlessness about her, but when she first got here she always seemed to burrow down into the house and the life here like someone wallowing in a feather bed. But before very long, Patti would be itching to move on. She would start to rail against the things she wanted to be a part of. She fought against me—and Booshie. Especially against Booshie. Then, that last summer she was here, both Patti and Barbara just happened to have yellow dresses, the brilliant harsh kind of yellow that hurts your eyes. One day Patti started to tease Booshie, who could never measure up, to her way of thinking. And she just happened to be wearing her yellow dress. She took Booshie's broom—the way she did today—and set off pandemonium. It was the day she was leaving, and Barbara never brought her again. But Booshie never forgot it."

I shivered.

Aunt Mercy went on. "But Booshie, knowing this the way she does know things, remembered Patti and remembered the yellow dress. She knew that all this had nothing to do with you."

Aunt Mercy didn't seem to expect me to say anything just then. "We'll talk more later on," she said, opening the car door and getting inside.

Patti didn't come to supper that night. I heard the telephone ring several times and the sound of her running to answer it. I heard Aunt Mercy talking to her in the study after supper: the tenor of their voices, but not the words themselves.

Later that night, when Patti came upstairs to bed, I held myself frozen straight, staring at the crack of light where the door was partway open, waiting for her to come in. I wanted her to come, and wanted her not to come.

And all the time I was wanting and not wanting, I wondered what she would say about what happened today, what I would say back.

But Patti went down the hall to her own room and closed the door.

sixteen

The next day started off as if the day before it had never existed.

Aunt Mercy and Booshie and I had breakfast together —just an everyday toast and marmalade kind of breakfast. Only the thing about it was that now we knew things about each other that we hadn't known before, and that knowing made us more comfortable with one another.

"I had Patti call Ethel Mae Cropper at the Light and Power Company yesterday afternoon," Aunt Mercy said as she cleared the table. "She can go back to her job tomorrow."

I took a long, deep breath. It was only then that I was able to remember that it was the Fourth of July and that the Firemen's Carnival was coming.

"Today's the carnival," I said.

"Three thousand and seven . . . three thousand and eight . . ." said Booshie, putting down her spoon and rocking back and forth.

"Booshie doesn't like all the lights and the noise. She won't go. But we'll go together after supper, the two of us. And stay for the fireworks," Aunt Mercy said.

"Three thousand and twenty . . ." said Booshie.

Later that morning, I went down to the vacant field across from the boardwalk and watched the workers set the carnival up. There were men stringing lights and loudspeakers and plastic pennants that flapped in the breeze; a tent rising clumsily in the middle of the lot, and a Ferris wheel where there had been only sky before. The merry-go-round spun emptily, and when someone tested the music of the calliope, I wanted to dance. I ran across the street and up on the boardwalk, looking back on the carnival grounds, squinting my eyes to see the way it was going to be. It was so exciting I wanted to share it with someone else, and for a minute I thought about running home, grabbing Patti by the hand, and dragging her back with me. Showing her the signs that said "Snow Balls . . . Cotton Candy . . . Hot Dogs . . ." To have her see the wheel games and the place the clown was supposed to sit balanced above a tub of water.

But in that split second between wanting to go and going I saw Patti and Booshie, and Patti pulling the broom out of Booshie's hands. I saw her doing the "Booshie sweep." I knew then that I couldn't go and get Patti. I went across to the corner, where a man was lining sawhorses

173

along the back of the booths, and walked next to him, so close that I could smell his sweat. So close that when he spit I had to jump.

I wondered if Patti would come with us tonight.

I thought that day would never end. It was as if the sun were stuck up in the sky; as if everyone were moving in slow motion. The heat built up until the air was tight and still.

As it turned out, I went to the carnival alone. Aunt Mercy called from the hospital to say that old Miss Birdy was worse and she would stay as long as she was needed. When Patti saw that it was just Booshie and me for supper, she got that funny trapped look on her face and pushed her food around her plate. When the phone rang, she went to answer it and never came back.

After supper, when Booshie was getting ready to do the dishes, she took the towels and clutched them to her chest and rocked back and forth, heel to toe, and motioned me toward the door, saying, "Go . . . go . . . go . . . go."

And I went. Straight down Mulberry Street. I waved to people sitting on their porches or just starting down their walks. I ran out into the street to pass the Tucker sisters and waved back at them as Miss Lily Tucker called, "You go along now, Henley, but save some cotton candy for us." I heard the music and moved faster, dancing almost, then looked back to see if anyone had seen me, then danced some more.

Cars were parked along the beach, and other cars and pickup trucks inched their way by, past fathers pushing babies in strollers and mothers holding on to the hands of other children pulling out in front; and women carrying cakes and folding chairs. Turning onto Bayside, I walked along next to Mr. Brown from the bank. I waved to Mr. Cropper, the shoemaker, and told Miss Ida Waters that Aunt Mercy was still up at the hospital.

Once onto the carnival lot, I was caught up in the surge of music and gave myself up to it, letting it carry me, like a wave carrying a beach ball, from place to place. I watched Mr. Trimper spin the wheel-of-fortune and saw a woman win a dozen eggs; and moved on to where Billy Parsons was having his picture done in charcoals; and stopped at the merry-go-round, feeling my stomach rise and fall with the circling horses. I stood on the ground beside the Ferris wheel and looked up and watched as the wheel jerked its way around while the seats were being filled, then caught my breath as the machine went spinning around and around. The sky behind the wheel was dark now and the carnival was rimmed with lights. Moving past the cake table, I stopped and watched children plucking plastic ducks out of water to see if they had won a prize. I smelled hot dogs and pizza and caramel popcorn and got in line for a root beer. I watched a little girl pulling cotton candy out of her eyebrows, and paid for my drink, while the lights and the music and the people swirled around me. I looked across the street at the sky over the beach and saw that the firemen had started to set off firecrackers, and watched the colors streak the sky—red, green, blue, gold— and heard the delayed booms.

The sand inside my sneakers gave my feet a slippery, gritty feeling. I stopped in front of a man standing on a barrel calling, "Right this way, folks. Right this way to

175

knock Bozo in the water. Three throws for a quarter. Come on, ladies and gents. Bozo needs a bath. Three for a quarter." I looked at the clown on the platform with his big leering mouth and his apple cheeks and I hugged my arms across my chest, laughing out loud as he leaned over and looked down at the tub of water beneath him and shuddered and wiped tears off his face. I edged my way up to the front, watching a boy throw three balls and miss. The crowd booed and rearranged itself, moving on to other things, but I stayed.

"Your turn, Gussie. You did it once before . . ."

"And won you an orange T-shirt . . ."

"With a tiger on the front . . ."

"With a plastic eye that rolled around inside . . ."

Looking sideways, I found myself standing next to the woman named Gussie, with her granddaughter just beyond her. I watched Gussie untie a bandanna and take out a quarter and hand it to the man. I saw her balance the three balls in her hand, weighing them one against the other, rubbing them with her knotted fingers. I saw her hand one ball to the girl beside her and heard her as she said, "One for my granddaughter, Mary Rose—Slug, I call her. And one for you."

I looked at the woman and at the ball she held out to me, and at Slug standing beside her, waiting.

"H, my name is Henley," I thought. "H—my name is Henley."

"My name is Henley," I said out loud.

"Dr. Mercy's girl," said Gussie, pushing the red ball toward me.

"Where have you been?" Patti shrieked, and the ball fell from somewhere between my hand and Gussie's and rolled across the sandy ground. "I've been all over this two-bit carnival a dozen times." She grabbed hold of my outstretched hand and pulled me away. "Come on. I've got to talk to you."

Patti lunged through the crowd, dragging me behind her, past the fortune-teller's booth and around the back of the merry-go-round to the edge of the lot. She let go of my hand and swung around to face me.

"There's not much time, I wasted so much looking for you. Just time for you to get back to the house and pick up a few things before the train."

"What train? Where are we going?" I felt the whole force of the carnival throbbing in back of me. I saw Patti outlined against the dark of the street and it was as if she were growing and growing, filling all the space where the beach should be.

"I told you we were getting out of here. That I'd had enough. I told you that the other day. It's all arranged. I've talked to Eric and he's found us an apartment. He has a lead on a job and everything's going to be okay. Come on, Henny-penny. We're taking the night train out of here."

"But, Patti . . ."

The music was suddenly louder: crashing and pounding and spiraling around us.

"There you go again—'But Patti . . . but Patti . . . but Patti . . .' I don't want to hear 'But Patti' or 'but' anything else. This time it's going to be different. Really okay. We'll get someplace terrific to live, and fix it up. There'll be money

—from the job Eric knows about. You'll see. Anyway, I'm not going to stand here in the middle of some rinky-dink carnival and tell you about it. You get yourself on back to Aunt Mercy's and pick up a few things right now. This time we're really traveling light. Leave it and we'll get all new." Patti moved toward me, and on past me, heading back into the center of the carnival, calling back over her shoulder, "Come on. Move it. I'm going over to the station and get the tickets. I want to have them in my hands for sure."

I watched Patti round the corner of a stand and disappear into the crowd. And suddenly I saw much more. I saw it the way it had been before, and the way I knew now it was always going to be. The moving, the searching, the running ahead of ourselves. Living here and living there. I saw Patti running after jobs and places and parties and friends that were always going to be better than the ones before. Except that they never were. I saw Patti chasing . . . chasing . . . chasing . . . Catching nothing. Not knowing what it was she never caught. And I knew that with Patti it was never going to be enough; that it was never going to end. I stood still for a moment and watched a rocket arching across the sky over the water; and I was that firecracker, going off, sending bits of myself streaking and crackling and splintering across the summer sky; until there was nothing left except the dark.

I started to run after Patti, calling her name and pushing past people, my feet slipping on the sandy ground. Back past the fortune-teller and the clown still poised above the water. I saw her just ahead of me.

"Patti, wait. Wait. I've got to tell you something."

Patti stopped and turned halfway around. I stopped

a few feet away from her and we stood facing one another, forming a pocket of space in the milling crowd.

"I'm not coming," I said. "Not coming anymore. Because if I do, then pretty soon there isn't going to be any of me left at all."

We stood frozen, staring at one another.

In that instant, from somewhere in back of us, came the sound of a gong and a cheering from the crowd and a loud splashing noise as the clown hit the water. The pattern was broken and the crowd surged between us.

Suddenly I was trapped there in that carnival. Bound all the way around by the music, the lights, the warm sweet smell of cotton candy. It was as though something were pulling backward at my feet so that I had to drag them one at a time—slowly at first, and then faster and faster. Forcing myself to move past the Ferris wheel and the hot-dog stand and the artist doing caricatures.

And, all around, Patti-faces looked down at me.

Patti-faces on the people riding the merry-go-round and eating ice cream and playing bingo. Patti-faces on the crowds that closed together whenever I thought I saw an opening. A way out.

The calliope whined and the firecrackers thudded against the sky. Bells rang and whistles blew and screams tumbled down around me.

I ran forward and then backward as all the Pattis thronged around me. I stopped and held on to the side of a ticket booth, trying to catch my breath. I felt someone near me—a kind of outline of myself. Moving and starting and stopping when I did.

179

I ducked under a counter and looked up at a shape in a white apron cooking hot dogs, and a Patti-face looked down at me. I crawled back out again.

Over my shoulder I saw the girl named Slug kneeling on the ground next to me. She stood when I stood, moved when I moved. Together we went across the carnival lot. Slowly. Slowly. And after a while the lights and the noise stopped spinning around me. The crowds thinned and moved back and had their plain everyday kind of faces on.

Slug moved behind me, without saying anything, and kept me going through the crowd to the other side of the lot, where there was now an opening between a van and the edges of a bingo game. I checked my watch and saw that more than half an hour had slipped by. It had gone in a flash. And it had taken forever.

Away from the carnival, it was dark and quiet, and we walked up Mulberry Street, past silent houses with wrap-around porches and trees and bushes out in front. The jangle of sounds in back of us got fainter and fainter.

As we got to the Presbyterian church, we heard the train whistle. I stopped, and Slug stopped with me. I think that, standing there in the dark and listening to the wail of the train, I knew for the very first time that Patti had gone.

We stood until we couldn't hear the whistle anymore, but only the noise of a bunch of dumb crickets rubbing their legs together the way crickets do, and then Slug pointed left and said, "I go this way now. I'll see you."

"Yeah," I said. "I'll see you," as I turned and went the rest of the way up Mulberry Street to Aunt Mercy's house.

seventeen

The days patterned themselves one after the other, and there was a sameness about them: heavy summer heat and endless time; the sound of lawn mowers, and a game of hide-and-seek on the next street over, and the sharp dry smell of grass.

There were trips to the store with Booshie, and to the hospital with Aunt Mercy to make her rounds, and to Fitchett Brothers' Second-Hand. Some days I went to the beach, and Slug was there. We swam together out past the diving pier and hunted shells and climbed out on the jetty. We talked some, but not much at first. The times we did talk, we heard what each other said, and what we meant to say.

Aunt Mercy's niece Barbara came from California and brought her two young daughters. I guess Aunt Mercy had

181

told her I was there, because she didn't seem surprised. The girls were okay, but they weren't much interested in the attic, even though Booshie and I took them up there. They mostly liked the beach and Barbara and I took them every day. One time, while they were in the water and Barbara and I were sitting on the sand, she told me some of how Patti was when she used to know her—the good things, anyway. How she was young and beautiful and full of life. I remembered that part of Patti. I remembered the other part, too.

I thought about my mother a lot. About why she was the way she was. And wondered if I would ever really understand it. I remembered Patti had told me I could do anything I wanted to do, be anything I wanted to be; and I was sorry she couldn't stand still long enough to see me do it. Because I knew by then that you could do things and still be in one place while you were doing them. But Patti didn't ever understand that, and maybe that's why she was all the time moving and going nowhere. I wondered if she would ever come back again. What would happen if she did. What would happen if she didn't. Patti was gone and I missed her. Somehow I knew that it was the kind of missing that would go on for a long, long time.

Aunt Mercy still played the piano, and Booshie counted and rocked and stroked her hand, and Raymond came to call.

My journal got fat and worn with all the things I put

in it: things that happened and things I made happen in my head.

Later on, there was a postcard from Patti from Atlantic City, and one from Florida. But they didn't say much of anything and there wasn't even a return address.

Down on Main Street, Gussie still trundled her wagon along, and Billy Parsons walked his dog, and Mr. Brown from the bank stood outside on the sidewalk and talked to whoever would listen. The fan in the ceiling of the Pop Shop went round and round, and Mr. Trimper put "back-to-school clothes" in the window of his store.

The days began to get shorter, so that some nights we couldn't sit on the porch as long as usual. When the wind came up and Aunt Mercy went inside to play the piano, Booshie and I went in with her and closed the door behind us.

One day Aunt Mercy took me to enroll in school and I was caught up in the smells that had been locked away there all summer. Chalk and apples and peanut butter. The same as in all the schools I'd ever been in, but somehow I had the feeling that this one was going to be different. As if it had been waiting for me.

The way this whole town seemed to have been waiting for me. The way it had already become the place where I belonged. There was one thing I would always remember:

183

it was Patti who brought me here.

The stuff of the Aunt Mercy stories reached out to take me in: the town with the beach and the water tower and the churches all around; the house with the swing on the front porch, the funny narrow back stairs, and the bathtub on feet.

And of course Booshie and Slug and Raymond and Aunt Mercy herself.

And me—Henley. I was a part of them.